"Aren't you forgetting something?"

He opened the door and took from the bottom shelf a single long-stemmed pink rose. He came back to her, his eyes teasing. "I told you I'd be checking."

Faith smiled, half apologetically, half ruefully, and reached for the flower. But the softening of Ken's eyes as he stood before her stopped the gesture. He took a step nearer, and Faith knew he was going to kiss her.

His lips would be soft and warm, like his hands. His kiss would be gentle, like the man. His taste would be sweet, like his smile. Although he hadn't touched her, already Faith could feel the kiss, already her senses blinded with the subtle shadows of quiescence. She forgot all the reasons she should not allow it to happen. She simply waited.

Books by Rebecca Flanders

HARLEQUIN AMERICAN ROMANCE

HARLEQUIN INTRIGUE

HARLEQUIN PRESENTS

HARLEQUIN ROMANCE

These books may be available at your local bookseller.

Don't miss any of our special offers. Write to us at the following address for information on our newest releases.

Harlequin Reader Service
P.O. Box 52040, Phoenix, AZ 85072-2040
Canadian address: P.O. Box 2800, Postal Station A,
5170 Yonge St., Willowdale, Ont. M2N 6J3

Rainbows and Unicorns

REBECCA FLANDERS

Harlequin Books

TORONTO • NEW YORK • LONDON
AMSTERDAM • PARIS • SYDNEY • HAMBURG
STOCKHOLM • ATHENS • TOKYO • MILAN

Published June 1985

First printing April 1985

ISBN 0-373-16105-0

Printed in Canada

Chapter One

Faith Hilliard had had only three kinds of days lately: bad, terrible and off the scale. This was one of the latter.

She was walking proof of Murphy's law, and since the hours had begun to tick down at the beginning of the week toward the biggest wedding of the year, everything that could go wrong had. The nursery had gotten the shipping date wrong on the invoice, with the result that two hundred unpotted lilies had arrived at Faith's shop three days early. She managed to crowd the flowers into her own closetlike greenhouse, but her humidifier had chosen that moment to go out. For the past three days her kitchen had been a tropical jungle, complete with bubbling vats of steam from simmering pots of water on the stove, hastily strung-up grow lights and the cloying smell of lilies permeating every inch of her house.

There were hourly phone calls from the mother of the bride. Faith wondered in despair how the estimable Mrs. Holt-Bancock possibly had time to oversee any of the other multitudinous details of the wedding when she spent all her time harassing the florist. She could not decide whether she wanted the corsages composed of pink or white sweetheart roses. Faith had finally ordered samples of both, made up two sets of corsages, and the good lady decided she wanted lilies of the valley. At the last minute she announced she wanted a floating centerpiece, complete with lighted candles, for the pool at the country club. Faith's distributors were going crazy, but they were nothing compared with Faith herself.

Faith knew she shouldn't have accepted such a big assignment. Her business was small, and so were her ambitions. She was perfectly content to arrange modest bouquets for birthdays and anniversaries; she kept her head above water with an occasional routine wedding or funeral. Mother's Day was always good for business. This wedding was far, far out of her league, and Faith could only assume that the reason she had been chosen over some of the larger florists around was because of her competitive prices—that, perhaps, and the wild promises she had made once she had started mentally toting up the profit. This wedding could mean the first time she had done more than break even since opening the shop two years ago. She couldn't turn down an opportunity like that.

The color scheme had been changed no less than three times since Mrs. Holt-Bancock had first met with Faith a month before, and sometimes Faith wryly cheered herself by comparing her plight with that of the poor dressmaker. And of course, nothing so simple as orange blossoms and carnations would do. Mrs. Holt-Bancock had run the gamut of every exotic and hard-to-find bloom in existence, and at one point had Faith in a panic when she decided upon a profusion of some rare Hawaiian plants as background foliage, which would have been difficult to preserve once they reached the heart of Indiana.

Fortunately, that, too, had been only a passing fad, but the final selection was not much better. Lilies and orchids, two of the most fragile blooms imaginable, were upon this seventeenth day of April to fill the auditorium of the church and assault the memories of the guests forever with their delicately musky scent, in honor of the union of Mary Beth Bancock and Jordon Stevenson.

Yes, it had been a rough week. Long hours at night and into the early morning arranging bouquets, corsages and baskets, days spent in teeth-clenching dread awaiting the next phone call from Mrs. Holt-Bancock or the distributor with a last-minute disastrous change of plans.... But today, the morning before the wedding, had been the final straw.

It hadn't been enough to wake up and find her cat contentedly munching at the carefully preserved lilies that still smothered Faith's kitchen. No real damage was done, but it was a bad omen for the day. Faith had all the lilies carefully wrapped in tissue paper and lovingly packed into the back of the van—and the van wouldn't start. The battery her mechanic had warned her about last winter had finally given up the ghost. Thirty long, fingernail-chewing minutes later the mechanic arrived, with many reproaches and a pair of jumper cables, and ten minutes after that, both Faith and her frazzled nerves arrived at the shop.

The first thing she noticed was that Sally, her assistant, had not opened up the shop as she had promised. It was deserted. The second thing Faith noticed was that the rose baskets, so painstakingly prepared the night before, were shriveled, blackened and frozen corpses. The cooling unit had gone berserk again. Dismissing the impulse to sit on the floor and break into tears, Faith got on the phone and scouted up a rush delivery of roses, then hurried to see what she could do to save the orchids, baby's breath and ferns. She was in the middle of throwing together another rose basket when Sally called. She claimed she had the flu; what she had was a hangover. Faith would have fired her on the spot but she simply didn't have time.

So now, three hours before the wedding, Faith was faced with the task of decorating the church and the country club all by herself, and she didn't know how she was going to do it. She just knew that somehow she would have to.

Faith's Flowers served three adjoining towns, none of them big enough to rate more than a dot on the map, and this wedding was in the little community of Twin Branch, about six miles north of the shop. Faith rarely made deliveries herself, so she was unfamiliar with this church. The first thing that struck her, as she pulled the van into the compact parking space near the side door, was how small the church was. She would have expected something much more elaborate for a wedding

such as this. The second thing she noticed was how
quaint it was, with its polished river-rock exterior and
diamond-shaped stained-glass windows—more like a
chapel than a cathedral, which was no doubt why Mrs.
Holt-Bancock had chosen it in the first place. The reception would be lavish and large, but the ceremony
itself was probably reserved only for family and closest
friends.

Faith got out of the van and made her way up the
short cobbled walkway, noticing with a wry grimace the
budding rosebushes at the door. If she had known
about those, she wouldn't have gone into such a panic
over the frozen flowers this morning. Then she observed philosophically that the day was hardly over,
and she might yet have need to rob the church's rose
garden.

As she had expected, Mrs. Holt-Bancock was already
there, along with several other key members of the
wedding party whom she ordered about with her usual
authoritarian aplomb, sending them to check on the
caterers, the cars, the musicians.... Faith smothered a
smile as she wondered which one of her scurrying ser-
vants was the groom, and if he had any idea what he
was getting himself into.

It took Faith fifteen minutes to assure the ubiquitous
lady, with a confidence she was far from feeling, that
everything was under control and on schedule. She
tried one more time to discourage her client from scattering the altar with rose petals—the petals would have
to be kept moist for the next three hours, and the
bride's gown would be irretrievably stained when she

knelt for the blessing—but the woman airily assured
Faith that all that was taken care of. Faith gave a re-
signed sigh and proceeded to spread the altar with a
waterproof sheet to protect the carpeting, and covered
it with hundreds of dollars' worth of rose petals.

Faith became absorbed in her work as the sanctuary,
through her efforts, began to take on the atmosphere
of the most solemn and joyous occasion of the human
celebration. Yes, she loved weddings—didn't everyone? But what touched Faith was not the sentimental-
ity and the symbolism attached to the event, but the
sheer beauty of it. The white gown, the pastel-colored
dresses of the bridesmaids, the graceful ceremony—
and of course, her own most treasured contribution,
the flowers. It often struck her how sad it was that all
this preparation, expense, attention to detail and lavish
beauty should go into the making of a ceremony that
lasted no more than fifteen minutes. By tomorrow
morning the gown would be packed away, the flowers
thrown out, and all the weeks of anticipation would be
no more than a memory. An actuality that was short-
lived, a memory that lingered... like a lot of things in
life, Faith supposed.

The easy part was done—the altar, the pulpit, the
windows all banked with flowers. The chains of pink-
and-white roses lining the aisles. The bridal bouquet
and corsages all neatly laid out in the dressing-room
refrigerator that was kept for just such purposes. Now
Faith began her real challenge—the weaving of two
hundred lilies and orchids into a double arch over the
vestibule.

She brought her stepladder, hammer, tacks and weaving materials into the church in two trips. Mrs. Holt-Bancock's courtiers were still scrambling at her command and did not offer to help a lowly florist. The arches, fashioned of wire, foam and stiff green paper from measurements Sally had given Faith at the beginning of the project, were heavy and unwieldy. They would be even more so when the flowers were added, and Faith could see no other solution than to fit the frames in place over the two natural arches in the vestibule, and do the actual flower weaving from the stepladder. At least the measurements were correct. That nemesis of an assistant of hers had done something right.

The background noise of echoing voices and strident commands faded into Faith's absorption with her work, into aching shoulders and arms and tender fingers as she steadily and rhythmically turned the ugly green hoops into a sensory delight of pastel colors and scent. Grudgingly, she had to admit that Mrs. Holt-Bancock's judgment had been on the mark—the combination of waxy white lilies and gossamer pink orchids against the background of verdant ferns was both exotic and delicate, a tantalizingly sensual array. The lush bridal bouquet was a reflection of the arches through which she would enter, the rose-strewn aisles matching the bridesmaids' bouquets. It was all, Faith had to admit, very striking and romantic.

An hour later, Faith could not believe that she had done it, all by herself...and just under the deadline. She surveyed her work with satisfaction, glanced at her watch to notice she had just twenty minutes to clean up and get out of there before the bride and her attendants arrived for the dressing process, and then climbed back up on the ladder to make one final quick adjustment to the arch nearest the door.

It had to happen. Faith could almost see it in slow motion before it even began. The door swinging open, knocking the stepladder from under her, Faith feeling herself beginning to fall, grabbing for the arch, tumbling to the stone floor with a thousand dollars' worth of flowers and labor toppling down with her, probably breaking her back and most certainly breaking her heart....

The door did swing open upon the entrance of a white-faced, teary-eyed young woman, and the edge of it did catch the ladder and throw Faith off-balance; she cried out and she did grab wildly for the arch to steady herself... but then she felt strong hands on her waist, and as the ladder clattered to the floor, she was being swung into a pair of healthy male arms.

Faith stared at him, her heart still tapping out its frantic rhythm of alarm and fear, her mouth still open to cry out in pain from the fall that never came, her eyes wide and shocked. And he looked at her, face crinkling warmly and green eyes dancing pleasantly, and he said, "Hi. I'm Ken Chapman, and I think I'm going to marry you."

Chapter Two

For the longest time—which was no more than seconds, actually—all Faith could do was stare up into those striking green eyes. They weren't exactly green, she noticed quite clearly, at least not in the sense of emeralds or forests or grass or any other of the natural elements one usually associates with the color. They were a crystal color, like certain Caribbean waters, or like cellophane tinted a very light aquamarine. Around the pupils was a perfect ring of gray, which was one of the most unusual configurations Faith had ever seen. It accentuated the dark centers and made his eyes look even larger, paler, almost transparent. It made Faith feel for one startling moment as though for the first time in her life she were looking directly into another person's soul, and that within that soul was a goodness so pure she could hardly bare to look at it.

It was seconds, a fraction of a millimeter in the row of hours and days and weeks and years that composed Faith's life, and later she would almost be able to laugh at herself for attaching so much significance to the moment. But later she would also notice that that moment flashed in her memory like a close-up photograph from an expensive camera, and she would be able to recall the minutest detail of his appearance, his dress, his scent, his feel.... But her senses were jolted back to the present in an instant as the young girl who had caused the accident rushed past them, unheeding and unapologetic, sobbing, "Mother—Mother, where are you?"

Faith began to struggle, gasping indignantly, "You most certainly are not! Put me down, please!"

The man blinked once, as though he, too, were just being nudged out of a reverie, and looked slightly confused as he set her obligingly on her feet. He glanced at the distraught young woman running toward Mrs. Holt-Bancock, then back to Faith with a grin. "You're..." He lifted a hand and before Faith could flinch away had lightly grasped the name tag on her smock, turning it so he could read it. He did not seem to be aware that the name tag rested directly over Faith's left breast, but Faith was, excruciatingly so. "Faith Hilliard," he murmured with a quirk of the brow. "Of Faith's Flowers." He dropped his hand and met her eyes, a veritable circus of amusement cavorting in his face. "I should have known."

On her feet now, Faith could tell that her rescuer in full body lived up to the promise in those unusual eyes. He could not be more than two inches taller than Faith, but his tight, lean build gave him the appearance of more stature than he actually possessed. He had a funny sort of face—and Faith would choose that word to describe it because there was simply no other. It was a face filled with pleasure and good humor, built for mischief and open appreciation of all life had to offer. There was a poetic gentleness there, a haunting sensuality, a capacity for endless delight in all pleasures, whether corporeal or ethereal. There was warmth, a startling genuineness that was rarely found anymore, a complete lack of guile. It was the kind of face in which one immediately recognized a friend, but beneath it was something else, a deeper quality that Faith thought could only be recognized by those trained, as she was, by crucial necessity to read a man's character in his face. It was a bedrock of toughness—not brutality, never that, but an underlayer of hard self-sufficiency, the mark of a survivor.

His hair, tousled carelessly over his forehead and around his ears, was dark brown with molten streaks of gold that captured the light from the stained-glass windows when he tilted his head back. His skin was a healthy burnished color, and Faith thought that with those eyes it would have been a disaster if he had been of fair complexion and blond; he would have looked like a ghost. He was dressed in navy tennis shorts, a red pullover and athletic shoes. And his eyes were still laughing at Faith unabashedly.

Faith scowled a little and opened her mouth to say something, but she did not know whether to thank him for his gallant and most opportune rescue, or to upbraid him for the impudent remark he had made once she was in his arms. In fact, she did neither, for at that moment her attention was distracted by the bride's sobbing in her mother's arms, the pitiful wail echoing and bouncing off the sanctuary walls, "O-oh—M-mother...something *terrible* has happened!"

Faith's eyes first widened with despair as they went to the huddle in the corner, then narrowed grimly, and her fists clenched against her hips in an unconscious thirst for vengeance. "If she's had a fight with her fiancé," Faith muttered tightly, "after all this work..."

Ken Chapman glanced at the source of the uproar, and the merriment in his eyes faded into a rueful shake of his head as he said, "I guess I'd better go see what I can do to calm things down." He glanced back at Faith, and the softness in his eyes, the sweetness in his half-smile, made her heart skip an absurd beat. "Are you all right?" he inquired, a little belatedly, and Faith found herself returning his smile in some confusion, and when she nodded she had no idea what she was agreeing to.

For just a moment longer his gaze met hers, and Faith thought there was a touch of reluctance in his face when he turned to cross the room toward the center of the dispute.

It took Faith less than a minute—but more time than it should have—to put the incident behind her and get her mind back on her work. In the background she heard the low tenor of Ken Chapman's soothing voice beneath the uproar, and out of the corner of her eye she saw him usher the little group out of the sanctuary and presumably into a back office. For a moment Faith hesitated, wondering whether she should wait to hear the outcome of the problem before investing any more effort in nuptial arrangements. Two things decided her:

First, with a family as volatile as this, even if the wedding were off now, it would no doubt be back on in five minutes. Second, for some strange reason, Faith had ultimate confidence in the diplomatic powers of Ken Chapman.

Besides, she convinced herself grimly as she swept up leaves and trimmings and gathered up her tools, wedding or no, Mrs. Holt-Bancock could rest assured that Miss Faith Hilliard would collect on her rather stupendous bill—whether or not the results of her labors were ever put to use.

She tried to keep her thoughts from wandering back to Ken Chapman, and she grew more irritated with herself as the task became more difficult. So what if he was an attractive man? She wasn't interested. There were thousands of attractive men wandering this earth, and the last thing she needed was one in her life. It was stupid to keep remembering how his arms had felt around her, holding her, supporting her in midair for just this briefest of times...insane to imagine, for even a second, that she needed or missed a human touch. Dangerously insane. Those eyes...cats' eyes, that's all they were. A freak of nature. And what kind of come-on was that—"I think I'm going to marry you"? Faith had been working too hard. Under normal circumstances she would have read him the riot act right then and there. Instead, she practically melted....

As she carried the last of her tools and her stepladder out into the April sunshine, Faith's arms and shoulders were reminding her painfully of the hour she'd spent on the ladder reaching over her head. She was looking forward to a long hot soak in the tub tonight, but first she had at least two hours' work at the country club... and she only prayed the van would start.

Faith heard the quick steps behind her a moment before the bulky aluminum ladder was lifted from her hands. She couldn't help flashing Ken Chapman a little smile of gratitude. His eyes in this light looked as clear as glass.

"The church looks great," he said. His smile seemed to go right through her body, and in that moment all of the stern lectures Faith had given herself on the disadvantages of being attracted to him were just wasted effort. He was attractive, she defended irritably. Why shouldn't she enjoy his company for a few minutes?

Faith laughed a little, pushing a flutter of straight light hair away from her cheek. "Thanks. It had better, for what they're paying me."

A network of lacy shadows passed over his face as they walked beneath a budding tree, and Faith noticed that the laugh lines surrounding his eyes actually began high on his cheekbone and spread outward. His skin had a rough, outdoorsy look. She wondered if its texture would be as coarse as it looked, or if it would be smooth, like the faces of most men in today's overcosmeticized society.

"Do you know the family?" he was asking, and again Faith laughed, somewhat nervously this time. She wondered if he had noticed how closely she had been scrutinizing him.

"Only the head tigress," she replied. She slid open the van door, and Ken tucked the ladder inside. Faith put the tools on the floor with a clatter and turned back to him, her eyes narrowed and sparkling in the late-afternoon sun. "That was more than enough for me," she confided. "What a tyrant!" She contained a melo-dramatic shudder.

Ken laughingly agreed. "Old Mabel's a trip, all right. I've unfortunately had a few run-ins with her myself. I'm sure there's a way to handle her but—" he gri-maced "—I haven't discovered it yet."

Faith could not imagine that there had yet been born the person Ken Chapman couldn't handle. She said, "I'm just glad it's over with... or at least, I hope it is." Faith glanced at him anxiously. "The wedding is still on, isn't it?"

He nodded, chuckling. "That little fracas in there was over nothing more than a pair of dyed-to-match shoes. Not to say," he added, holding up thumb and forefinger a mere fraction of an inch apart, "that they didn't come this close to calling the whole thing off. Fortunately for all concerned, cooler heads prevailed. Will you have dinner with me tonight?"

It came so much as a natural part of the conversation that for a moment Faith didn't even hear him. For yet another moment she was completely nonplussed. The cool aplomb that was usually within fingertip's reach on such occasions deserted her completely and she practi-cally stammered, "You have a wedding to attend."

"I'll be finished by seven-thirty, time for a quick cos-tume change and on your doorstep by eight. I hope you like pizza," he added, perfectly bland. "I'm not a rich man."

Faith stared at him as he leaned negligently against the side of the van in tennis shorts, his hair ruffled by the wind, his eyes blindingly clear, and her first absurd impulse was to say yes. So startled was she by this instinct that she was thrown completely off-balance. She searched around frantically in her mind for something to say, and what finally came out was, "The wedding party is from South Bend, aren't they? I always wondered what made them decide to hold the ceremony in a little town like this."

Ken did not take his eyes off her. Faith thought a person could eventually wilt under the steadiness of a gaze like that. "The groom is my brother-in-law," he offered, as though that explained everything. And it did. Far too well. "Most of the family originated here. You didn't answer my question."

Faith was careful not to let a flicker of expression cross her face. Married. She should have guessed. Some things never changed.

Faith closed and locked the sliding panel in two deliberate motions. "Thank you for your help, Mr. Chapman," she said pleasantly. She brushed past him without a glance. "Have a nice day." Faith opened the van door and climbed inside.

He looked completely bewildered. "Hey, wait a minute...."

Faith slammed the door and turned the ignition key. The engine, mercifully, started, and she backed the van out of the parking space.

She couldn't resist glancing at him, just for a second, in the rearview mirror as she pulled out of the church parking lot, and it was a move she was going to regret. The picture of him, standing in a pattern of sun and shadow looking very confused, would haunt her the rest of the day.

FAITH WEARILY CLOSED the door to her house an hour after dusk that evening, and then simply leaned against it, closing her eyes, too tired to take another step. Her shoulders burned magnificently now. She would be sore the rest of the week.

Two more disasters had crowned the day, and Faith considered herself fortunate, the way her luck was running, to have gotten off that easily.

The first was rather minor, involving a squabble with the chef over the fact that her design of rosebud garlands on the table was distracting attention from his exquisitely carved radish rosettes. The argument would have passed unnoticed had not Faith, in a fit of clumsiness no doubt generated by the cumulative tensions of the week, accidentally knocked his rosettes to the floor and squashed a few under her hastily retreating feet. The repercussions of that fiasco threatened to reach as far as Mrs. Holt-Bancock herself, had not the chef wisely remembered just in time that even his temper could not compete with his employer's, and when an irate mother was summoned from her daughter's wedding half an hour before the ceremony, it would not be so much a matter of who was to blame as who was the easiest target. The chef decided not to take the chance and went grumblingly back to the kitchen, leaving Faith only a little worse for wear.

Twenty minutes before the reception was scheduled to begin everything was perfect. The country club reeked of lilies and candlewax, white lace and roses. It looked like something out of a French film, all bows and flower blossoms and soft lighting. The string quartet was warming up in a fern-screened corner, the wedding cake presided majestically over the center table surrounded by a carpet of rose blossoms. And then the anchor that held Faith's magnificent floating centerpiece in the pool broke loose, threatening to upend the six-foot-wide work of art, candles and all, into the chlorinated water. Faith had no choice but to make a grab for it...and, naturally, she fell in. She saved the centerpiece, though, and at that point a good soaking was the least of her problems.

She was aching, soggy, chilled and exhausted. But it was over. At last, the worst week of her life was over.

A strident yowl at her feet prompted Faith to open her eyes a crack, looking downward into the scowling topaz eyes of a very disgruntled tomcat. She returned his glare ounce for ounce, and finally warned distinctly, "Don't start with me, Lancelot. I have not had a good day."

The cat made a formidable opponent sitting there at her feet, his paws spread and his haunches flared aggressively, ready to pounce or at least give her a firm reminder who was boss if Faith did not acquiesce to his will. He was a ragged-looking animal, with all the raw-boned grace of a mountain lion and almost as many scars. He had a coat that looked as though every color known to feline had been scrambled together in a blender and poured out in no particular pattern to cover his body, and eyes that glared to kill. He had come with the house when Faith moved in two years earlier and immediately made it evident that she was here only by his grace—not the other way around. They lived in perfect harmony as long as Faith remembered two rules: Lancelot expected his meals to be served on time, and under no circumstances was his freedom to be curtailed.

Faith eventually relented under his accusatory gaze and pushed away from the door, mumbling, "All right, all right. I don't know what the big deal is, anyway. You knew I had to work late today."

She trudged across the room toward the kitchen, flipping on lights as she went, and her tennis shoes squeaked soggily. Faith's two-bedroom saltbox house was a charming clapboard structure on the outside, meticulously landscaped and painted Williamsburg blue with white trim and shutters for contrast. It gave the entire neighborhood a touch of old-fashioned class. On the inside it was hopelessly disorganized. Tiffany and hurricane lamps mixed with a contemporary sofa and beanbag chairs. Art deco posters competed with landscape prints on the walls. None of the colors matched. Lush green plants crowded up every inch of living space, and the prevailing decorating scheme was clutter. Magazines, books and collectibles were scattered at random. An enormous teacher's desk served as part bar, part china closet and part catchall. A wrought-iron bench reposed against one wall and an antique sewing-machine cabinet decorated another. Faith had furnished her home with whatever struck her fancy, and her tastes were eclectic.

The sink was piled with a week's worth of dirty dishes, but the thought of washing them tonight overwhelmed Faith. She opened the cabinet and stared into it sightlessly for a moment. She had not had time to do any shopping this week, either. "You're in luck," she murmured after a moment, and discovered the last can of Little Friskies hiding in a corner. She found the can opener after some searching and dumped the contents of the can into her last clean bowl. For a moment with her hands on her hips, she watched Lancelot dive into his dinner, then she commented dryly, "Please, go ahead and start without me. I have to change, anyway."

Faith was too tired to even draw the bath her body ached for. She simply shrugged out of the wet clothes and into a warm blue terry wrapper and fuzzy slippers, towel-dried her limp, fine hair to a dull sheen, and then felt a little better as she went back into the kitchen.

"So," she inquired of Lancelot, who was still busily devouring his dinner, "how did things go around here today? Catch any good mice? Read any good books?" She gave the cat a disparaging glance. "You're not much of a conversationalist tonight, are you? It's very bad manners to gulp your food." She found a jar of dill pickles in the refrigerator and a jar of peanut butter in the cabinet, and opened them both. "My day was pure hell," she said. "Thank you for asking. Sally called in sick again. I've got to do something about her."

Faith took both jars into the living room and slumped down on the sofa, resting her feet on the coffee table.

After a moment Lancelot, replete, followed her. Faith was too tired to even turn on the stereo or the television set. She was almost too tired to eat.

Lancelot jumped up on the sofa, sat down beside her and began to lick his paws. Faith dipped a pickle in the peanut butter jar and took a bite. "One interesting thing did happen, though," she mused, munching. "I met a man...a nice man." Then she shrugged, dipping the pickle again. "Or at least I thought he was nice. Turns out he was married, and coming on to me like you wouldn't believe." Faith did not understand why she was still thinking about Ken Chapman—but more, she did not understand how her judgment could have failed her so badly. She was generally razor-sharp when it came to assessing a man's character. But it had been a long time, and perhaps she was getting rusty.... She laughed a little, dryly. "Right in a church parking lot, too, with his friends and family all around. Some people have no class."

She took another bite of the peanut-butter pickle, chewing thoughtfully. She was remembering the way the wind had played with his dark hair and the laugh lines that deepened toward his temples. There was a faded freckle at the corner of his left cheekbone and a sprinkling of them across the hollow of his throat. She suddenly gave Lancelot, who had paused in his washing to stare at her, a dark glance. "You needn't look at me like that," she informed the cat. "I know the score."

She dipped the last half-inch of her pickle into the peanut butter, popped it into her mouth and licked her fingers. "But I didn't tell you about his eyes," she went on, frowning a little with the memory. "He had the funniest eyes I've ever seen. I can't even describe them, they were so weird." But it wasn't just the color of the eyes, it was the character behind them...the pureness, the openness, the calm confidence...or maybe she was just fantasizing.

She took out another pickle and looked at Lancelot closely. Ken Chapman's eyes weren't like cats' eyes, after all. They were quite simply in a category by themselves.

She shrugged it off, dipping the pickle into the peanut butter. "I know what you're thinking," she went on in an uninterested tone. "That if he hadn't been married I might have gone out with him. Well," she declared firmly, crunching down on the pickle, "you're wrong. What do I need with that mess? I never needed it before, I don't need it now, I'm not interested. End of subject." Lancelot met her determined stare unblinkingly, and then responded with a loud yowl.

Faith frowned. "A lot you know," she muttered. She speared the peanut butter with the pickle and set the jar on the coffee table. "Come on, you're going to be late for your date."

She got up and crossed the room to the back door; Lancelot followed her in a moment. "Don't keep her out too late," she advised wryly as she opened the door and Lancelot marched sedately through it. She muttered to his retreating tail, "Ungrateful wretch," and closed the door firmly behind him.

She wandered back into the living room and sat down, curling her feet beneath her on the sofa this time. In a minute she would get up and take that bath, then go immediately to bed. The prospect sounded absolutely heavenly after the week she had had, and it deserved to be savored for a time.

For a moment she rested her head on her folded arms and thought of absolutely nothing, but eventually the trials and tribulations of the day came snaking back. Faith frowned a little as she remembered Sally's treachery, and she reached for her pickle. She had been so busy all day that she hadn't even had time to be angry, but this really was the last straw. When the girl worked, she worked well, but what good was any employee if she could not be depended upon? With the wedding over and Mother's Day almost a month away, business would be light for a while. If she had managed this awful day with no assistance, Faith could surely handle anything else that came up by herself. She would be well advised to inform Miss Sally Perkins firmly and in no uncertain terms that her services were no longer needed as of first thing tomorrow morning. . . .

The strident ringing of her old-fashioned, twist-type doorbell startled Faith out of her reverie, and her scowl deepened. Speak of the devil. . . . If that was Sally thinking she could make things right at this late date, the young lady was in for the surprise of her life. Faith was not likely to ever be caught in a more unforgiving mood.

She stuck her pickle in the peanut-butter jar again, wiped her hands on her robe, and went to the door. She turned on the porch light and, out of habit, peeked through the window. She could see a figure but no face, and she cautiously opened the door to the length of its chain.

"All right," said Ken Chapman easily, "so you don't like pizza. I'm sure we can work out some compromise."

Faith caught her breath and instinctively pushed against the door, only to feel it lodge against an object at its base—his shoe. She looked down, startled, at the foot that was wedged between door and frame, and then back at him again, and Ken gave her a modest grin. "I used to be a door-to-door salesman," he explained.

Faith did not like to be caught off-guard. It always confused her. Her mind was racing, and it was such a tangle of half emotion and half reason that she didn't even know what she was thinking. He should be at the reception. He shouldn't be here. How had he found her? Didn't the man know how to take no for an answer, for goodness' sake? Didn't he have any moral sense or loyalty to his wife whatsoever? Why had he picked on her? And beneath all this, which confused Faith even more, was a very definite pinpricking leap of excitement, and it even felt a good deal like pleasure.

But Faith would not succumb to any of these irrational thoughts because above them all, one was very clear. She would not be used for a one-night fling by an out-of-town wedding guest, and it infuriated her that he would think she could. It more than infuriated her. It touched a white-hot rage deep within her that was born purely of vulnerability. It made her feel as though her carefully fashioned mask had been ripped away and exposed her naked before his eyes, and she hated him for that.

She said coldly, leaning against the door, "You have exactly thirty seconds to get off my porch, Mr. Chapman, and then I'm calling the police."

The humor swiftly left his eyes, leaving them only stripped and confused. But he did not remove his foot. "Look," he said quietly, "I'm not trying to harass you. Maybe I misread things this afternoon—" and those quick light eyes seemed to probe her "—but I don't think so. If I've done something to offend you, please tell me, but all I wanted was to ask you to dinner."

Faith took a deep, quiet breath. How could he be so sincere, so gentle...and how could she almost fall for it? Still her voice was very cool, though she lightened her weight a little against the door. "I don't date, Mr. Chapman," she explained simply. "Especially married men." And she started to close the door.

His hand came up swiftly to grasp the edge of the door, and his eyes were wide with surprise. "Married?" he echoed. "Who told you a thing like that?"

Faith looked pointedly at his hand. "You did," she replied evenly, and applied a little more pressure to the door. It didn't budge.

"I did no such thing," he objected strenuously, and his forehead creased with concern and confusion. "What made you think..."

Faith braced her hip against the door, preparing to slam it. "Men with brothers-in-law generally have wives," she explained tersely, and again fixed her eyes on his hand. "Move it or lose it, Mr. Chapman."

He did neither. He merely stood there looking at her with astonishment and growing amusement bubbling in his eyes, and he replied calmly, "Men with brothers-in-law also sometimes have sisters. Is that what this is all about?" The merry incredulity was practically snapping in his eyes now. "Jordon Stevenson is my sister's husband's brother. The family is so close-knit, I've always treated Jordon like another brother-in-law. How could I be married," he insisted endearingly, "when I've already told you I'm going to marry you?"

Faith stared at him, her lips parted speechlessly for a long moment of spiraling and cavorting thoughts and realizations. He wasn't married. Her judgment had been right after all—he had sought her out. The sincerity she had seen in those window-clear green eyes had not been imagined after all...but he was outrageous, presumptuous and possibly even dangerous.

Faith said flatly, "You're crazy," and started to close the door again.

He had relaxed his grip on the door and removed his foot, and she had almost closed the door in his face before he caught it again, fingers wedged tightly between door and frame. In the narrow crack that remained Faith could not see his face, but his voice sounded pained. "Miss Hilliard," he said patiently, "you may find this hard to believe, but I'm really a very shy man. You can't imagine the courage it took for me to look up your address and come out here in the middle of the night with no invitation and very little encouragement from you—"

"No encouragement," Faith interrupted tersely, but

already her lips were beginning to quirk at his soulful and unabashedly fabricated tale. "None whatsoever."

"I can appreciate the fact that I may have offended you with my forwardness," he continued formally, "but is it really necessary to make your point by depriving me of the use of three fingers on my most important hand?"

Faith could no longer repress her smile. She opened the door wide enough for him to free his hand, closed it again to remove the chain, and then opened it wide enough for her to place her body between the door frame and the living room. He smiled at her.

He was wearing a chocolate-brown corduroy sports jacket and a pale blue shirt that was open at the throat. He obviously hadn't just stopped by on his way to the reception—he had changed clothes after the wedding and come especially to see Faith. She was touched by that, a little guilty over her previous treatment of him, and for some reason uneasy. She half suspected he was serious.

She said quickly, before he could steer the conversation onto a more personal level, "How was the wedding?"

"Beautiful," he answered. She could see his eyes flicker over her once from head to toe, and she was suddenly embarrassed by the bulky bathrobe and scruffy slippers. But he seemed to find nothing displeasing in her appearance. In fact, in the split second his eyes were away from her face, they seemed to have grown even warmer. "Like all weddings. It went off without a hitch, and your flowers made the show. All the guests were oohing and aahing over them."

He had found her weakness, and Faith couldn't help smiling. Any man who complimented her work couldn't be all bad. She said, "Why aren't you at the reception?"

One eyebrow lifted as though the question were absurd. "Why, because I had a date with you, of course."

Faith stiffened her muscles and took a deep breath. Why was she suddenly finding it so difficult to hurt his feelings? It had never bothered her with any other man. But this one was not like any other man. She actually found herself starting to apologize. "Mr. Chapman—"

"Ken," he corrected easily.

"Mr. Chapman," Faith continued stubbornly, "I'm sorry if you got the wrong..."

But his eyes had wandered over her shoulder to examine the contents of her living room, and he interrupted, wrinkling his nose, "Pickles and peanut butter? Is that dinner? Maybe I should have gone for the pizza after all." Then he looked back at her pleasantly. "I'm sorry. You were saying?"

He obviously did not intend to make this easy. Faith took another breath. "I was saying," she stated clearly, "that I'm—flattered by your attention...." Was that she, Faith Hilliard, uttering those ridiculously polite words? Flattered by your attention. "But—I don't go out. I don't date. At all." There. It sounded silly and stilted, and it embarrassed Faith to hear the echo of her own words, but she could hardly put it any more plainly.

Ken Chapman looked unimpressed. "That's a pity," he observed mildly. "You see, I'm a rather old-fashioned kind of guy, and I believe in a good, solid courtship before rushing to the altar. That's going to be somewhat difficult if you don't date."

Faith was not at all certain he was teasing. "Hi, I think I'm going to marry you" was an original line, she had to give him that, but he was beginning to run it into the ground. And because she simply couldn't be sure exactly how seriously he took himself, she was uneasy.

"You're crazy," Faith decided, and started to close the door.

He reached out a hand, not to stop her, but to lean casually against the door frame, his fingers spread a few inches away from her terry-covered arm. His smile was relaxed, and kind. "No, I'm not crazy," he said gently. "But you're obviously tired and ready for bed, so I won't bother you anymore tonight. I would like to know, though, if you don't mind—is there a particular reason why you don't date?"

There was no flippancy in his tone; in fact, Faith could detect nothing but a sincere interest, a genuine curiosity that was only natural under the circumstances, she supposed. He made her want to answer him.

Faith swallowed hard. "Yes," she said. "A personal one."

He straightened up, and a slight curve of his lips acquiesced to her need for privacy—for now. But he said,

"It will be interesting to find out what it is...some-day." And his smile deepened. "Good night, then, Faith."

Faith watched him turn and go down the walk, and she heard herself murmuring dazedly, "Good night."

Chapter Three

"I don't get it," Faith complained to Lancelot the next morning, wincing as she tugged a comb through her stubbornly tangled hair. "You spend the night slinking through alleys and crawling through sewers and you look as good as you ever did. I spend ten hours in bed and I look like..." She gave a final grimace as she freed the last tangle. "Well, like I've been doing what you have."

But Faith knew what her problem was. Those ten hours in bed had not been spent sleeping. As exhausted as she was, her restless mind simply would not be still. And most of it was Ken Chapman's fault.

Her eyes were bloodshot, and there was a delicate blue discoloration beneath them that only emphasized the paleness of her skin. Faith was fair-complected and delicately constructed—tall, thin and fragile-looking. A pound lost on her could look like ten, a couple of nights' restless sleep would make her eyes look like those of a prizefighter who had lost the last round. Stress made her lips pale, her skin pasty and her hair limp. Under ordinary circumstances Faith would have paid little or no attention to what she looked like, but today it irritated her that her haggard appearance would announce to the world that she was under stress.

Her straight, shoulder-length hair was a fine blend of shades of blond and pale copper that varied its tint, like a chameleon, according to the light. Once Faith had enhanced that effect with a light red rinse, but she didn't bother anymore. Once she had spent a fortune on weekly hairdressing to maintain that natural, casually straight look; now she discovered it was just as natural-looking—and a lot cheaper—to take a pair of scissors to her dead ends once a month. Generally Faith wore her hair tied back at the nape with a scarf or a rubber band, but today she wanted to wear it loose. And, of course, today it hung around her face as limp and lifeless as an old dishcloth.

Similarly, Faith never troubled herself with makeup anymore, although her collection of cosmetics would have put Helena Rubenstein to shame. But today she was certain her wan and battered appearance would scare the customers away, so she diligently began to rub on rouge and lip gloss, applying a heavy coat of cover stick under her eyes and blending a line of sea-green shadow into the crease of her lids. That helped—the cover stick was surely the most blessed device ever invented by woman, and the faint green shadow gave some life to her worn-out hazel eyes. But there was absolutely nothing she could do about her hair. Resignedly, she snapped it back into a rubber band, and went to make Lancelot's breakfast.

She had even dreamed about Ken Chapman. Him and his haunting green eyes...how long had it been since she had dreamed about a man?

"Who am I kidding?" Faith muttered with a snort of laughter as she flung open the cabinet door. "I've never dreamed about a man."

All right, so he had made an impression. There was nothing to marvel at over that. He was striking, unusual, vibrant—he could not help but make an impression on everyone he met. And it wasn't every day that Faith received a personal visit from a persistent suitor who declared within two seconds of meeting her that he was going to marry her, and stuck to the story, too.

Faith smiled a little indulgently, stirring a cup of instant coffee as Lancelot settled down to his breakfast. Fortunately, the cat wasn't a picky eater, and he seemed to be thoroughly enjoying the cold cereal and milk Faith had served him. She shrugged and sat down at the kitchen table across from Lancelot, defending out loud, "So it was romantic. Nothing wrong with that." She took a sip of the coffee, absently watching Lancelot. She was not aware that her lips curved into a vague, almost wistful smile. "I mean, let's face it, old boy, I'm twenty-eight years old and the only brushes with romance I've had have been slightly less than memorable. Naturally I miss it. Not—" she assured herself with a quick nod in Lancelot's direction "—that I'm in the market. But if I ever were, I'd want it to be done right this time. Flowers, candy, poetry..." And a man with fascinating gray-rimmed eyes and a gentle smile orchestrating it all? She laughed and finished off her coffee. "Fat chance, eh, Lance?" She grabbed her purse and headed for the door, calling over her shoulder, "Cat food—I won't forget. Why don't you earn your keep around here today for a change, huh? Do the dishes or something!"

The cat lifted his face from the cereal bowl, with milk frothing his whiskers and a look that could have killed, and Faith laughed as she locked the door behind her.

DESPITE THE ROUGH NIGHT, Faith was absolutely determined to put an end to the miserable luck that had assailed her this past week. The worst was over, and the stars or the planets or whatever it was that had been plaguing her had surely moved on by now to darken someone else's life. She didn't even despair when her engine whined and moaned for a good thirty seconds before finally coughing into life, but took the whims of fate into her own hands and made her first stop that morning at the garage, where she had a new battery promptly installed.

Sally was late once again, and as Faith drove up the repair crew she had ordered for her cooling and humidifying systems was just driving away. With much frantic blowing of her horn and waving, Faith managed to flag them down, and she was so relieved to have caught them that she forgot to be mad at Sally for not opening up on time.

Now Faith could concentrate on recuperating from disaster and rebuilding in the aftermath, and she found her spirits steadily rising as she settled down to the routine. The repairs would be completed by midafternoon, so she began to make calls to restock her inventory. She spent the morning preparing an itemized bill for Mrs. Holt-Bancock, and that definitely boosted her morale. Sally wandered in while Faith was working in the back room, putting together the spring arrangement of dried flower baskets, and Faith put down her work calmly and went to greet her. She knew exactly what she had to do. It only amazed her that she had put it off this long.

Faith came out into the front room, her hands in the pockets of her smock, and said casually, "You're late."

Sally turned to her as she slipped on her own smock, wide-eyed. "I told you I was sick," she whined. "I only dragged myself in here today because I felt guilty about leaving you alone...."

Still Faith was very calm. "You didn't seem to worry about that yesterday."

For a moment Sally looked utterly baffled, and then her expression graduated into the horror of utter chagrin. Whatever else the young lady was, she was a good actress. "The wedding!" she gasped. "I forgot!"

Sally would have stood a far better chance had she simply admitted her failing and accepted the responsibility. This kind of grand deception insulted Faith's intelligence and completely exasperated her patience.

"You forgot," Faith returned dryly, "the most important wedding of the year, the only thing we've been working on, day and night, for the past month."

Sally knew she had made a mistake. She grew defensive. "Now listen, Miss Hilliard..."

"No, you listen, Sally." Faith could be tough when she had to. It was a side of her very few people ever saw, a side that Faith diligently tried to keep hidden, but she thought of her aching shoulders and the nightmare that was yesterday; of all the things that could have gone wrong and all the things that had, and she finally got angry. The time for second chances was over. "You've been working for me for six months, and in that time you've been late forty-seven days and 'out sick' fifty-two." Faith also had a memory for details, and that little-known fact registered first as shock, then as resentment in Sally's eyes. Faith kept her hands bunched in her pockets and her tone even as she clipped out the sentences. But her face was that of a woman who has reached the end of her patience, and Sally could see the ax start to fall. "This cannot go on. I run a business here, not a—"

The clanging of the bell over the door announced the arrival of a customer, and Faith drew in her breath sharply, cursing silently. Sally's face was swept with quick relief and she said hastily, "I'll take care of it," and beat a swift retreat across the room, out of reach of her employer's wrath.

Faith did not turn around as she heard Sally inquire cheerfully, "May I help you, sir?" Sure, Faith thought, all sweetness and light now that she's gotten a reprieve. She tightened her fists in her pockets and began to count to ten, fighting the urge to drag Sally away from the customer and finish what she had started. Sally would be avoiding her like the plague for the rest of the day, and who knew when Faith would be able to work up enough righteous indignation to start the whole speech over again.

And then she whirled around as a masculine voice, which by now was as familiar as her own, replied, "I'd like to see the proprietor, please."

It was Ken Chapman.

Faith could not help but be aware of a sudden increase in the tempo of her pulse that seemed to send a rush of warmth to her cheeks; she hoped it was not visible. There was a tingling sensation in the pit of her stomach that felt like nervousness and she deliberately tried to ignore the pattering sound her heart made inside her chest as she went over to him.

"I'll take care of this, Sally," Faith told the girl. "You go in back and start on those flower baskets."

Sally gave her employer a suspicious, almost resentful look, but she was not about to push her luck. She did as she was told.

For a moment they just looked at each other. Ken was dressed today almost as casually as he had been when Faith had first seen him: in jeans, sneakers and an open-throated yellow pullover top. Faith could see that pale pattern of freckles rising from his collarbone, and the light covering of golden-brown hair on his forearms that she remembered so well from yesterday, when those arms had been around her. She could see the curve of his breast muscles defined by the clinging material of the shirt—not a broad chest, but a strong one. The luminescent color of the shirt seemed to be caught in the sunshine that poured through the front window and lightened his hair, and his eyes were almost silver. He was smiling at her, and Faith had never noticed before how bright and airy her shop was until he stood there in that sweep of sunshine from the window, smiling at her.

Faith said evenly, keeping her voice pleasantly professional, "You don't know when to give up, do you?"

Ken's eyes wandered downward to rest just briefly in the region of Faith's collarbone, and she had the absurd impression that he could actually see the pulse that had suddenly leapt there. And his quiet, patient smile never wavered. "This is purely a professional call," he assured her in the same polite tone she had used. "I want to place an order."

Faith accepted that somewhat skeptically, and it showed in her eyes as she led the way to the counter. Amusement sparked in his.

The workmen clattered and fussed with the cooling unit behind her, traffic passed lazily up and down the street before her, an occasional face would register in the window to admire her displays. But for Faith there was nothing and no one within the scope of her senses except Ken Chapman, leaning his bare forearm casually on the countertop, the fresh, woodsy scent of his cologne drifting toward her, bright eyes watching her every move. She fumbled with her order pad, dropped her pen, felt a blotchy color creeping up from her collar, and grew more irritated with herself by the minute. And all the while she could feel his gaze, a palpable thing, falling over her—warm, gentle, a little amused, robbing her of concentration and wreaking havoc with her professional composure.

Finally Faith got both pad and pencil in order, scrawled his name across the top, and she was even more annoyed with herself because she did not have the courage to trust what was left of her composure to meet his eyes. She demanded without looking up, "Address?"

"Seven twenty-eight Pharr Street, Little Creek."

Now Faith looked up in surprise. "You live here?"

And she saw a reflection of her own surprise in his eyes as he replied with a lift of an eyebrow, "Of course."

Faith busily scribbled out the address, feeling foolish for some reason—as though she should have known his address simply because he had assumed she knew it. She chattered nervously, "I—I guess I was under the impression you were only in town for the wedding...." But she had been under a lot of false impressions about him, from the beginning.

She felt, rather than saw, that warm humor in Ken's eyes, as though he knew the reason for her sudden attack of nerves and sympathized with it, but nonetheless found it amusing. "No, it was the wedding party who came to me," he explained patiently. "I told you that, remember?"

He must have. Of course he had. That brother-in-law business. Faith thought he must be fairly important to the Holt-Bancocks for them to move an entire wedding for his convenience, but then he had said most of the family had originated here, too, and it was really none of her concern.

She took a breath, reorganized herself, and looked

up at him pleasantly, in control now. "And what did you want to order? My inventory hasn't come in yet," she felt compelled to explain, just as she would to any other customer. "As you can see—" she gestured behind her to the workmen "—I'm having some repairs done, but I'll have a full stock this afternoon, and you can certainly look through my catalog and order anything you like. Of course, we have some beautiful arrangements of dried and silk flowers—"

"That won't be necessary," he interrupted smoothly. He seemed to find fascinating the movements of her face and her hands as she talked. "I know what I want."

Faith had the distinct impression that Ken Chapman always knew what he wanted.

For a split second she let her eyes be captured by his, then she forcefully snapped her attention back to the business at hand. "Fine," she said. Her smile was practiced. "What will it be?"

"Roses."

Faith barely stifled a groan in time. She didn't care if she never saw another rose, but at least he hadn't ordered lilies. It occurred to Faith to wonder for the first time who was important enough in his life to deserve roses. But it was only a transient curiosity, not to be examined—possibly because she was half afraid, even then, that she knew the answer.

She tried not to let her smile waver, and she inquired, "Do you know what type you want?"

"Yes," he replied without hesitation, as of course he would. He never took his eyes off her. Faith got the impression that all the time he had been standing here, leaning so casually against the counter and conducting ordinary business, those strange, high-powered eyes had been acting like some sort of X ray, scanning and examining her innermost layers and deepest secrets. The only reason that suspicion did not terrify Faith was because it was such a gentle assessment, such a bland and neutral probing. It did not terrify her, but it made her very nervous. "I want," Ken Chapman said, "a single long-stemmed silver-pink bud to be delivered every day until I tell you to stop."

Faith stared at him. She hardly had any need to ask, but she did anyway. "To... whom," she managed, "do you want these delivered?"

He answered without blinking, "Miss Faith Hilliard, Fourteen thirty-four Apple Valley Lane, Little Creek, Indiana."

Faith let the pen drop; she met his innocent gaze steadily. "Not funny, Mr. Chapman," she said coolly.

"No joke, Miss Hilliard," he returned politely, and he reached for his wallet. "I'd like to pay a month in advance. Would you make up a bill, please?"

It was no use. She simply could not stare him down. "This is ridiculous," she informed him, and was unable to keep the exasperation out of her voice or the embarrassment out of her face. "And it's totally unnecessary. I can't let you..."

He merely lifted an eyebrow. "I believe I heard you tell your assistant only moments ago that you're running a business here. Well, are you or aren't you?"

She took a short, frustrated breath. "I will not," she

informed him through clenched teeth, "deliver flowers to myself!"

He seemed to contemplate that. "The next nearest florist is in South Bend. It seems to me it would save trouble all around if you accepted the order, but if you don't want to..." He shrugged.

He was serious. He was really going to do this, and nothing Faith could say or do would dissuade him. Of course it was unethical to take his money, of course it was ridiculous... but it would be only slightly less embarrassing than having a fancy florist's truck from South Bend pull up at her house every evening to deliver a single pink rose to the local florist. With one final dark, frustrated look, Faith began to total up the bill. All right, she would take his order. She'd take his money and it would serve him right.

"I'd like to write a card, too," he added mildly.

Faith did not look up. "The cards are on the counter," she snapped.

Thirty long-stemmed roses. Faith wondered grimly if Kenneth Chapman had any idea how much this little practical joke was going to cost him. Maybe when he saw the bill the whole problem would be solved.

"That will be ninety-three dollars and ninety-six cents," she told him, looking up, "with tax." And then, because he was looking at her so patiently, so sincerely and so completely unsurprised, she felt compelled to add, somewhat disgruntledly, "I didn't charge you for delivery." She had also charged him wholesale, but she didn't tell him that. It was only a stupid impulse of conscience that had made her do it, anyway, and she would probably regret it. She should have charged him retail and enjoyed it.

Ken counted out five twenty-dollar bills, and Faith turned to make his change. This was absurd. Completely absurd. What was he trying to do, anyway? Win her affection by boosting her business? Or was he really, truly, certifiably crazy?

She counted out his change, and he looked at her steadily. "I want the roses delivered to Miss Hilliard's home," he told her plainly, "not her place of business. Every day. I'll be checking on it."

The corners of Faith's mouth tightened as she plopped the last penny into his hand. That sounded very much like a promise to plague her for the next thirty days, at least. What was she going to have to do to get rid of this character?

And was she really all that sure she wanted to?

"The card," Ken said, and handed it to her. "To be included with the first delivery."

Faith pocketed the card and kept her expression blank.

The suddenness of his smile dazzled her. "Have you eaten lunch?" he asked.

Faith blinked, once, as though trying to rid her eyes of the effects of a flash of light, which was exactly how his abrupt changes of mood affected her. "N-no. That is," she recovered herself sufficiently to add, "I don't eat lunch."

His eyes swept her slim figure once, and though it was a perfectly friendly, almost impersonal glance, Faith had to fight a ridiculous urge to close her smock around her at the collar. She felt her skin tingle with what she hoped desperately was not a blush. "That's obvious," he agreed cheerfully, and he met her eyes again. "I don't suppose you'd let me take you to lunch today?"

Faith shook her head automatically. "I told you, I don't..."

But Ken was already nodding, anticipating her answer. He straightened up and turned for the door. "See you later, then."

Faith looked after him just until the bell clanged on his exit, then she turned quickly and took out the card.

"A single pink rose," it read, "—for hope."

Faith's expression softened into a mixture of tenderness and despair, and she simply held the card, reading and rereading it for a long time. He was serious. And what was she supposed to do about it?

But that wasn't the real problem. The fact was that she was enjoying this—the attention, the sentiment, the...romance. Bizarre as some of Ken Chapman's tendencies might be, he fascinated her. Worse than that, she liked him. She didn't even know the man, but she had liked him from the very moment she had landed in his arms when, in that peculiar instant of unguarded insight, she had looked into his eyes and imagined she saw all sorts of things never dreamed of before. And now this note. For hope. What was she supposed to do? How was she supposed to feel?

She didn't know what she was supposed to do, but she did know how she felt—moved, elated, bubbly inside and a little light-headed, tingling and girlish, happy. Shy. Nervous. Confused. But also a little worried.

Faith folded the card and put it slowly back into her pocket. She really shouldn't let this go on. She should refund Ken's money and refuse the order, and she should make it clear to him that she was not interested. But maybe that was her whole problem. Maybe she *was* interested.

In what, she demanded of herself scornfully. Hearts and flowers, moonlight and champagne, sweet nothings whispered in her ear? Having a love affair? Getting involved with a man? Whom was she kidding? So Ken Chapman had swept her off her feet briefly with those strange light eyes and charming smile and a little attention... but "briefly" was the key word. All right, the attention had been flattering, the break in her routine exciting, the illusion of romance a little titillating, but it went no further than that. Faith was a sensible woman who knew what she wanted. And she did not want anything else that Ken Chapman had to offer. He had already caused her enough inconvenience with those stupid roses.

Feeling very pleased with the firmness of her decision, Faith turned her attention back to her work and resolved not to give Ken Chapman and his foolish extravagance a second thought.

That, of course, was much easier said than done.

Chapter Four

Faith had not counted upon the persistent unpredictability of the man she had determined to ignore. And there was absolutely no reason for the weak, melting sensation to start flowing through Faith's chest when Ken Chapman reentered the shop a scant twenty minutes later.

He crossed the floor at a bright, easy gait, holding up a brown paper bag as he stopped before the counter. "Sandwiches," he announced cheerfully, "direct from Graumann's Drug. Where can we eat?"

Faith looked at him in helpless silence. The man was too much. He had just spent ninety-three dollars and ninety-six cents to keep her supplied with silver-pink roses for a month, and it didn't even get him a lunch date, so what did he do? He went out and brought lunch to her, and did Faith really think she could order him out of her shop now? Of course she knew she should put a stop to this, of course she knew she shouldn't encourage him, but he was absolutely irrepressible. He had brought lunch; what harm could it do to share a sandwich with him?

Faith's lips gradually began to tighten into a smile that was part exasperation, part resignation and part helpless amusement. "This way," she said, and led the way to the back room.

Sally had not budged since being assigned to the flower-basket task almost an hour ago, but the look she gave Faith when they entered the workroom was not a happy one. In fact, it was positively disgruntled. "It's almost one o'clock," she complained, getting to her feet stiffly and rubbing her chapped fingers. "Could I have my lunch break now? I'm starved. And look at my hands." She held out her hands to Faith as though she actually expected sympathy, but all she got from Faith was incredulity.

"Lunch break!" The beginning of a temper crackled in Faith's voice. "You just got here! You—"

But then she remembered Ken right beside her, and she had no wish to air personal confrontations before strangers. She released an impatient breath and made a swift dismissing gesture. "Go on," she said shortly. "But be back here in half an hour."

Sally's cheerful nod meant that she would be back in an hour, and she scooted from the room.

"Employee problems?" Ken asked as he helped her clear the work table of dried straw, silk leaves and foam clippings.

Faith shrugged. "Sally's not the most reliable assistant I've ever had," she admitted. "And—" Faith stacked a pair of clippers beside the pile of straw they had swept to the end of the table and pulled up another chair "—I don't think I can put up with it much longer.

I'm going to have to look for someone else. Do you want coffee?'' She kept a pot going in the workroom all day.

"I don't use drugs," he responded, and seeing her startled expression, Ken explained, "Caffeine. This is much better for you." He pulled out two cartons of milk. "Cups?"

Faith retrieved the Styrofoam cups while he unpacked the sandwiches, both of them enormous, delicious-smelling club sandwiches—a ham, cheese and turkey for her, a Reuben for himself. "And," he said with a grin, holding up a waxed-paper cone, "a dill pickle. I gather you have a weakness for them."

Faith laughed and accepted the pickle, and the light in his eyes deepened as he caught a glimpse of the sparkle in hers. That made Faith feel shy again.

Faith had never been hungry at lunchtime, and despite the perfectly built, freshly made sandwich, she didn't possibly see how he could expect her to eat it all, drink the milk, and have any room left over for the pickle. She took a few token bites of the sandwich and a sip or two of milk, and then started munching on the only thing she really wanted—the pickle.

Of course her lack of appetite was not entirely due to habit. It was very difficult to concentrate on food in this totally alien situation—a man sharing lunch with her in the back room of her own shop—and his presence caused a tightening in her stomach that could have been nervousness or it could have been excitement. The room was sweet with the spicy potpourri of dried flowers and sunshine through a dusty windowpane, and

Faith's eyes kept wandering to the angle of his arm as he lifted the sandwich to his mouth, or to the strong-boned wrist, or to the way his hair curled around his ear and the tiny crease on the back of his neck. The sounds of the workmen in the other room were muted, and Sally must have put the Closed sign on the door because no customers came in. Even the telephone did not ring. There was a closet of intimacy surrounding them, formed by the spicy-scented air and the shared meal and the shadows of light that fell over them in the tiny room, but it wasn't entirely threatening. It was in many ways almost pleasant.

Ken glanced at her barely touched sandwich and lifted an eyebrow disapprovingly. But all he said was, "At least drink your milk."

Faith stifled a giggle and lifted her cup. "Yes, mother."

Again, there was that sweet lightening of his eyes, a soft appreciation that seemed to brush across his face just a moment before his lips curved into a subtle smile. Again Faith felt as though he were seeing directly into her soul. She quickly lowered her eyes and took a sip of her milk. After the pickle, it tasted unbearably bitter, but she tried not to grimace.

Ken wiped his fingers on his napkin and sat back, watching her. "I'm thirty-two years old," he announced, "in disgustingly good health, no major body scars or false parts; I play tennis and racquetball and swim three miles a week. I don't smoke, drink or swear—although I have been known to slip on an off-color joke or two."

Faith watched him cautiously, taking another sip of her milk. She hardly noticed the taste this time.

"I barely scraped through college," Ken continued implacably, "but I did much better in my postgraduate work, when I was older and wiser. I make less than twenty thousand a year, but I have good prospects. I like the Three Stooges, Edgar Allan Poe and sunsets. My childhood ambition was to be an opera star, but I can't sing. My father is retired from the railroad, my mother is still a church pianist. They've been happily married for thirty-six years. My only sister, as you already know, is married to Jordon Stevenson's brother and lives in South Bend with her husband and two-year-old son—they've been blissfully happy for five years. I was born in Battle Creek, Michigan—yes, people really do live there—and it was a nice place to grow up in, except for the winters, which are very, very cold. My grandfather worked in the steel mills, and his father was a farmer, his father before him—"

Faith had to interrupt, a little breathlessly, "what are you doing?"

He looked innocent. "Why, just giving you the minimal information you need to have about the man who is about to offer you a lifetime of happiness."

Faith lowered her cup carefully, and this time she refused to flinch from his gaze. She wanted to be stern with him, but it was very hard to do while looking into a face that was so deliberately arranged in endearing lines. More than that, she really found his entire approach so refreshing and charming that her only inclination was to play along with him. But Faith had long since grown out of games.

"Ken," she said, as severely as she could manage, "cute is cute, but I'm beginning to find this whole thing a little less than amusing. Now, you're a very nice man, and I might even like to be friends with you—" had she said that, had she really said that? "—but you've got to stop this nonsense about marrying me. It's embarrassing."

She expected a mock display of injured sensibilities or a dramatic protest of undying devotion; she expected a swift and unaffected witticism so typical of his quirky sense of humor, she expected to be smiling at herself and at him and putting up with his nonsense tolerantly—and enjoyably—for the next thirty minutes. She expected anything but the sudden soft curve of an absent smile, the slow tilt of his head, the quiet, steady gaze. The way he looked at her made her breath stop, made her mind reel, made everything, for one crazy moment, seem to slip and tilt on the axis of sensibility, and it made her almost believe in him. He looked at her with a quiet wisdom and a simple sincerity that saw and understood things far beyond her range of vision, and he merely said, "Is it nonsense?"

"O-of course it is." The slight stammer in her voice robbed her of the conviction she had meant to inject. In fact, looking into those patient, untroubled eyes, she had difficulty convincing herself. "I mean—" she absently began to tear the crust off her sandwich "—you can't just go around picking up women off the street and deciding to marry them—that's uncivilized! And also silly."

Now there was a spark in his eyes, and Faith could not be sure that it was not gently mocking her for taking his little joke so seriously. "I didn't pick you up off the street," he pointed out. "You fell right into my arms—like a gift from heaven."

Faith felt a prickle in her cheeks; she lowered her eyes and continued to tear the crusts of her sandwich. "You know what I mean," she muttered uncomfortably.

But he was serious again. "Don't you have room in your life for the unorthodox, Faith?" he inquired. "The unexpected moment, the little twists of Fate, the Unseen Hand that guides our lives in the directions we least expected to go?" His lips smiled gently, but his eyes were quite sober. "With a name like yours, surely you believe in miracles?" he inquired softly.

Faith cleared her throat a little, very uncomfortable now. Her fingers were busily making bread crumbs out of her sandwich, and she could not meet his eyes. His voice, his presence, the very warmth of his body seemed to hover around her and gradually enfold her in an embrace that was sweeter, more intimate and more pervasive than the physical hold of arms. And the worst part of it was that Faith wanted to snuggle into that embrace, to let it surround her and fill her, to rest secure within the spell he wove. "No," she said, in a low voice. "No, I don't believe in miracles."

She could feel the steady, undemanding strength of his gaze, and she refused to meet it. But it bore down on her, it crept into her, it seemed to hook itself around something very basic in the core of her and draw her to him. And just when Faith thought she could not stand it any longer, Ken's hand came out and his forefinger curved lightly beneath her chin, lifting her face to a level with his.

His touch was unexpected, and perhaps that was why it seemed so momentous. She noticed irrationally how soft his fingertip was, smooth and uncalloused, and how warm. Though the pressure was almost infinitesimal, she could feel the imprint of his finger on her skin, and she could imagine that small circle of warmth lingering in a tingling brand of sensation long after Ken had removed his hand. He touched her, and she looked at him, and though the distance of the worktable separated them, something of him seemed to flow into her and connect. His quiet, smiling eyes caught hers, and Faith could not look away. She no longer wanted to. "So," he asked, very gently, "do you really think I'm crazy?"

How could she look into those subtly compelling eyes, that kind, unaffected face, and lie, or evade, or be facetious? Her voice was a little husky, not far above a whisper. "No," she said, and admitted for the first time to herself it was true. "No, I don't think you're crazy." Only the most intriguing, unusual, perfectly captivating person she had ever met.

Satisfied, he dropped his hand and sat back, still watching her with lively, soul-absorbing interest. "What do you do first thing in the morning?" he demanded unexpectedly.

Faith caught a startled laugh. "What?"

He leaned back in his chair, arms folded across his chest with his hands tucked into his armpits, his expression alert and friendly. "Are you a day person or a night person?'' he insisted. "Is it hard for you to get up in the morning or easy? What do you do first thing?''

For a moment Faith merely looked at him, confused, guarded and half-amused, but then her own sense of fun got the best of her and she replied pertly, "Brush my teeth. I can't stand to start the day with a dirty mouth." His eyes sparked in quick appreciation, and she continued easily, "I'm neither a morning person nor a night person. My personal biorhythm peaks at somewhere between noon and six o'clock in the evening. I hate getting up in the morning, but if I stay awake past midnight I get nauseated."

"And then what do you do?" he inquired. "After you brush your teeth, then what?"

Faith's eyes crinkled with skeptical amusement, but she was beginning to enjoy this. "I shower, get dressed, feed Lance—my cat—drink a cup of coffee, and go to work."

"And then?" he encouraged. "You open up the shop, flip the sign over, and...?"

Faith's face was a mixture of curious amusement and coyness—an expression so rare that it would have amazed Faith herself could she have seen it. It delighted Ken. "What are you, an undercover reporter for *People* or something? Am I going to wake up tomorrow and find my life's story splashed across America's breakfast table? Why are you doing this?"

The way Ken's smile lit in his eyes just a split second before it played with the corners of his mouth fascinated Faith. "I'm just trying to find out," he answered her, "what it is that makes you the very special person you are."

It might have been nothing more than a conventional phrase, a pat conversational reply that was merely one among his store of dozens, but it startled Faith. Like so much else that he said and did, that simple sentiment reached out to her, touched her, took on a significance that was as wonderful as it was unexpected. To a man like Ken Chapman everyone would be a special person. But no one had ever said, or implied, that to Faith before. She had never, in her entire life, considered herself special or even very valuable—until she looked into Ken Chapman's eyes. The sudden self-enlightenment was rather sad, and confusing.

And it was also unforgivably sentimental.

Faith shrugged, sipping her milk again. "I'm a pretty dull character. Nothing very interesting about me at all."

A trail of mischief scampered across Ken's eyes, and he opened his mouth to reply, but a stern "hrummph" from the doorway made them both look up.

"Have to send to South Bend for a part, Miz Hilliard." The larger part of the two-man work crew that had been commissioned to repair her cooler lumbered over to her, invoice in hand. "Need you to sign right here. Got to keep her unplugged over the weekend, but we'll be back first thing Monday morning."

Faith stared at him, the pen he had given her suspended in midair over the paper. "What do you mean—unplugged? You can't leave it unplugged—I have a shipment coming in this afternoon!"

"Sorry, ma'am." He did not appear to be the least bit sorry. "You plug it in, and it's only gonna frost over and blow the motor before we get back out here, then you may as well order a whole new unit, which ain't a bad idea come to think of it—that one can't have six, seven more months left in her. We got your humidifier fixed, though," he added, as though fully expecting that to cheer her up.

Faith simply looked at him in dismay. Of the two, she would rather have had the cooler operating.

"Isn't there some way you can patch it together," Ken inquired, "until the new part comes in?"

Intelligent question, Faith thought in a mixture of gratitude and annoyance. She should have thought of it.

But it didn't matter. The man simply shrugged again. "Quittin' time's two o'clock on Saturday. Union rules. Back on the job nine A.M. Monday. Just sign here, ma'am."

Faith didn't know what else to do. Could her refrigerator at home possibly hold two dozen roses, three dozen carnations, an abundance of ferns and greenery, eighteen gladiolus—she almost groaned out loud. The gladiolus were enormous. A half-dozen irises, a flat of daisies... but what else could she do?

She glanced at her watch as the big man plodded out of the room. It might not be too late to stop the shipment.

But it was, she discovered three minutes later, hanging up the workroom extension. The truck had already left on its route.

She cleaned away the lunch leftovers and came back into the front room just as the workmen were leaving. Her mind was frantically trying to negotiate the logistics of storing a week's worth of inventory in a twelve-cubic-foot refrigerator, and at first she didn't notice Ken getting to his feet beside the cooler.

"Well," he announced cheerfully, dusting off his hands, "another stroke of luck. Instead of your having to recite to me detail by detail the events of a day in the life of Faith Hilliard, I get to stay here and observe firsthand."

Faith blinked slowly, focusing with difficulty from her present dilemma to his merry meanderings, and he explained with a dismissing gesture in the direction of the cooler, "I can rig that thing together so it will hold the weekend. Those guys could have done it a lot faster, of course, but—" he shrugged "—union rules are union rules."

"You're a cooler repairman?" Faith inquired skeptically.

He grinned. "Only part-time. Don't worry," he assured her airily, "I was first in my auto-mechanics class in high school. All it will take is a quick trip to the hardware store. Back in a minute."

"But this is not a car!" Faith called after him—but too late. The doorbell clanged on his exit.

Her skepticism faded into amusement as Ken returned fifteen minutes later armed with a roll of duct tape, a pipe wrench, a gallon of antifreeze and a bagful of miscellanea Faith could not identify, and proceeded immediately to stretch out before the cooler at her feet

as though he had every confidence in the world that he
knew what he was doing. Her despair evaporated into
careless laissez-faire beneath the distractions of his
banging and clattering with the pipes and incessant conversation, while Faith attempted to wait on customers
and take telephone orders and generally conduct her
business in a semiorderly fashion.

Sally was allowed only one curious glance at the unusual repairman before she was banished again to the
back room and the flower baskets, and between customers Ken would shoot such questions to Faith as,
"Where did you go to grammar school?" and "What
was the name of your very first boyfriend?" and
"What's your favorite color?" Some of the questions
were whimsical, some serious, some slightly sugges-
tive, but before Faith knew it she was falling into the
spirit of the game. Whatever else Ken Chapman was,
he was an expert at human relations. He knew that
there was nothing women—or men—liked better than
to talk about themselves, and though it was a trick
Faith had discovered long ago and used thousands of
times, she had never expected to have it used on her.
She was surprised at how eagerly she fell for it. She was
surprised at how much she enjoyed it.

Never had an afternoon flown by so quickly. No one
before had ever expressed such an interest in the mun-
dane elements that composed the woman who was
Faith Hilliard, and he drew her out so skillfully, so
easily, that she would be amazed to look back later and
discover that within the course of that brief afternoon
she had practically told Ken Chapman the story of her

life. He learned about her childhood in Des Moines, Iowa, her very ordinary parents who still lived there. She told him about the redheaded, freckle-faced boy with two missing front teeth who had, in the third grade, pledged his undying love in exchange for her roller-skate key. She told him about her winning year as a member of the Southside High girls' basketball team and about three fruitless years of violin lessons between the ages of twelve and fifteen. He learned that she was allergic to gold alloys and strawberries, that she wore flannel pajamas with feet in the wintertime and could recount the plot of every "Star Trek" episode ever made. He told her, lying on his back with a pipe wrench propped up against his chest, that she had very pretty legs. That made Faith feel silly because her first instinct was to move away, and he chuckled when she did.

She told him about her abortive attempt at Illinois State—with a few salient details omitted—and about her decision to open a flower shop in a small town two years ago. Little Creek had been chosen because it was the first small town Faith had come to. The years between the time she had dropped out of college and the time she had arrived in Little Creek were deliberately skimmed over.

Ken never seemed to get tired of hearing her talk, and just when Faith had decided this had gone on long enough and that even if he claimed she was not boring him she was certainly boring herself, he would make some perceptive observation or ask some thoughtful question, and Faith found herself telling Ken things she had never told anyone before...mostly because no one had ever asked. He wanted to know what she thought about everything, from world politics and current events to philosophy, literature, films and music. And because "What do you think" was another question Faith rarely heard, she answered with a wealth of opinions and preferences.

And neither was he devoid of opinions. He was as quick to disagree with her or point out failings in her logic as he was to applaud her choices, but Ken never lingered on one subject long enough for Faith to explore an intellect that promised to be as absorbing and impressive as his lightning personality. He was tasting, sampling and exploring her, opening and marking avenues that would be returned to for further discovery, and Faith found the process as delightful as it was amusing, and totally irresistible. *Why*, she thought at one point, *you're almost as easy to talk to as Lance*. And that brought a giggle to her lips, whose source Ken was never to discover, as hard as he tried.

And wonder of wonders, he actually fixed the cooling unit. Faith had to trust him on the complicated technical details as he tried to explain to her just how he had rigged the unit to maintain a constant temperature for the next thirty-six hours, but because he did not seem the least bit intimidated when she threatened him with a lawsuit if she came in Monday morning and found her entire week's inventory locked in ice cubes or wilted with heat, she felt confident enough to place the fate of the entire flower supply of Little Creek in his hands.

Sally went home at five-thirty on the dot, pointedly turning the sign on the door to Closed as she did, and Ken and Faith were left to arrange the last of the flowers in the newly rejuvenated cooler. "Well," Ken declared in evident self-satisfaction, closing the door at last on a wisp of temperature-controlled air, "now do you believe in miracles?"

Faith spared one last cynical glance for the noisily humming cooling unit. "I prefer to reserve judgment until Monday," she decided.

They were standing very close in the small space between the cooler and the counter; Faith did not realize how close until she looked up and saw him looking at her. Their bodies were almost brushing. Their eyes were on a direct level. She could have imagined it, but she almost thought she felt his breath whisper across her cheek. The natural thing for Faith to do at that moment would have been to step casually away, thanking him for his help and reaching for her purse and shop keys. But she didn't. She met that quiet, tender, absorbing gaze, and she let it work its magic on her. She did not move.

And inevitably, as she surely must have expected, his hands came up to touch her. They cupped her face very lightly. "If you could see what I see," he said softly, "you would believe."

The sounds of small-town rush hour outside the door faded away, the crunch of tires, the squeak of brakes, the laughing voices passing by the window blended into a buzzing background with the clunking hum of the cooling unit and the suddenly distinct pumping sounds of Faith's heart. His hands made her skin tingle, but it was more than just the physical touch that drew her and subdued her and surprised her with its arresting power. It was more than just chemistry. It was something about the fact that it was he, Ken, who was touching her, Faith. It was something about the way he looked at her. Maybe it was no more than the sweetness of the gesture, the simplicity of his hands cupped around her face, caressing it and examining it, as though that were the most important part of her to him.

"What...do you see?" Faith had to ask, and her voice was a little husky.

The slight softening of Ken's lips was not quite a smile. It was more of an inner wonder, a secret delight that crept to the surface without his being aware of it, and it slowly took Faith's breath away. "I see," he answered, and his thumb very lightly stroked the corner of her eye, "a woman who is all simple lines and beautiful architecture on the outside, a clutter of disorganization and contradictory styles on the inside—like a certain Williamsburg blue house on the corner of Apple Valley Lane and Lemon Drive." His lips quirked provocatively as he felt her uncertain blush. "I see peanut butter and pickles and piles and piles of white lilies. I see a very fragile young lady who somewhere along the way had to learn to be tough." His voice softened, and his eyes followed the movements of his forefinger as he gently traced the shadowy blueness beneath her eyes. "I see eyes that are older than they have any right to be; secrets, and shattered dreams, a little bit of fear, and maybe, now, just the slightest beginnings of what might be the awakening of hope. But mostly—" and his hand left her face to whisper over the shape of her head, his fingers barely touching her hair, as though he were tracing her aura in the air "—I see great beauty, simple and strong, the kind that comes from deep inside." And slowly he let his hands drop until they were resting with a feather touch on her shoulders. He smiled. "That's something I don't see very often," he said quietly.

For just a moment the spell lingered, and then the misery of reality came seeping and bubbling out of the corners, spreading its foul stain over the exquisite tapestry of fantasy he had woven. Beauty. Simplicity. Strength. Faith had none of those things. He did not know her.

Faith dropped her eyes; she moved imperceptibly away. The absence of his hands on her shoulders felt like a chill. She wanted to tell him he was wrong, that there was nothing pure or simple or good about her; she wanted to tell him to stop wasting his pretty words and his ineffable charm because she was not falling for it; she wanted to say something crass and ugly to shock him or something flip to discourage him; she wanted to be angry with him because, without meaning to, he had hurt her.

But it was as though he had read her face, or her thoughts, because before she had a chance to work up the necessary emotions or even try to form the damning phrase, Ken said easily, "What do you have for dinner?"

Faith was so used to answering his questions by now that she replied automatically, moving past him for the shop keys, "Stir-fried vegetables." And then she stopped, her hand midway to the hook on the back wall, and thought, *Oh, no. You've just given him the perfect opportunity to invite himself over, or...*

But he only said, eyes warm with a subtle, almost teasing, light, "Perfect choice. Very healthful." And Faith relaxed. "Have you ever considered," he inquired as she bent to retrieve her purse from beneath the counter, "playing classical music in here for your potted plants? It works wonders."

Faith straightened up slowly, trying to disguise another skeptical look. "I don't believe in things like that. The right balance of chemicals, water and light is all you need for a healthy plant."

"Try it," Ken advised with an enigmatic lift of his brow. "You might be surprised."

Faith checked the back room to make sure the lights were off, the thermostat was set, and the coffeepot unplugged, and Ken was still waiting for her when she came out. Faith was half nervous, half anticipatory for the scene that was about to follow. Ken had spent the day with her. Faith had enjoyed every minute, as hard as she had tried not to. Wasn't it only natural, then, that something more should be said than "good night"? They weren't strangers anymore. Would he ask to see her again? Would he offer to drive her home, or even ask her out to dinner? Would he... would he perhaps try to kiss her? After the strangely intimate scene that had occurred between them only minutes ago, it seemed more than likely. But if Faith had learned anything about Ken Chapman today, it was that he was not predictable.

Her smile was an uncertain mixture of businesslike dismissal and friendly gratitude as she said, "Well, thanks for your help. I don't know how I would have managed without it." And she gave a little laugh. "Assuming, of course, that you haven't been lying all the time about your auto shop course and I don't walk into an igloo in here Monday morning."

"Didn't I mention?" A mild smile lit his eyes as he watched her cross the room and touch the switch to dampen the overhead lights. "I don't lie. Another one of my absurdly self-righteous virtues."

The room was lit only by the shadow of fluorescent grow lights and a pinkish sunset that spilled through the front window. The cooler coughed and sputtered reassuringly. Ken stood between a display of potted geraniums and a shelf of lacy spring flower baskets, and the contrast of bright pinks and reds and pale pastels was muted in the indirect lighting, seeming to blend into a swirl of gentle color of which he was the center. Soft-edged patterns of light illuminated his skin, and the sunset warmed his face. Faith felt something tighten in her chest as she looked at him, as he simply stood there, watching her, and she tried to dismiss it with a quick, tight smile as she moved toward the door.

When she was within six inches of him, she felt the expected touch of his hand on her arm, stopping her. But it was not for the reason she had supposed. She looked up at him with a mixture of anxiety and anticipation leaping to her eyes. She was certain he noticed the ridiculous catch of her breath, but all he said was a mild, "Aren't you forgetting something?"

Faith started breathing again as he left her to cross silently to the cooler. He opened the door and took from the bottom shelf a single long-stemmed pink rose. He came back to her, his eyes teasing. "I told you I'd be checking."

Faith smiled, half apologetically, half ruefully, and reached for it. But the softening of his eyes as he stood before her stopped the gesture. He took a step nearer, and Faith knew he was going to kiss her. His lips would be soft, and warm, like his hands. His kiss would be gentle, like the man. His taste would be sweet, like his smile. Already Faith could feel it, already her senses were blinding her with the subtle shadows of quiescence. She forgot all the reasons she should not allow it to happen. She simply waited.

Ken brought the rosebud to her cheek, stroking lightly. The dewy cool texture of it felt like velvet against her skin, its subtle fragrance enfolded her, a sensory thrill that made her want to tip her head back in sheer pleasure, turning her face to receive more, to close her eyes and revel in the sensation. His smile was more in his eyes than on his lips and hardly there at all, almost like a memory. It was warm, and tender, and deeply absorbing, and it held her mesmerized.

The full, lush body of the rose traced the path his lips might have taken, slowly, gracefully, hypnotically. Across her forehead, brushing her eyelids, down the gentle slope of her nose. Outlining the curve of her lips. Again. And again. Faith was hardly breathing. She could hear her heart rushing and waning in her ears, and her fingertips tingled, yearning for something to tighten around. The rose traveled downward, caressing her chin, her throat, the open triangle of flesh exposed beneath her collar. She shivered as the cool, moist bud nestled for a moment against the button that closed the material over her breasts, and there was a warm weakness in her knees that seemed to be generated from no more than the intensity in Ken's eyes.

And then he smiled, and dropped the rose to her hand, curling her fingers around its stem. He held her closed hand with the rose in his, then he turned her hand over, his eyes dropping to study the delicate pattern of pale blue veins on her wrist that his thumb lightly traced. Faith could feel her pulse tripping rapidly against the almost infinitesimal pressure he generated there.

"The substance of things hoped for," he said softly, and he looked at her, smiling. "The evidence of things not seen."

He lifted their joined hands and placed a soft, warm, infinitely tender kiss on the sensitive underside of her wrist. And he said simply, "Good night, Faith," before he turned and left.

Chapter Five

The next day was Sunday, and Ken did not call. Filled with restless energy the night before, Faith had done her shopping, housework and laundry in record time and nothing remained to occupy her Sunday morning. She made Lance a festive breakfast of poached eggs and sausage links and lingered over the morning paper. By ten o'clock, she found herself glancing more often than she would have liked toward the silent telephone.

"It's not that I want him to call," she defended herself to the scornful yellow-eyed stare of the cat. It was just that she had expected him to call. Faith knew human nature, and all the signs were there. Ken Chapman was not a person who was going to disappear aimlessly out of her life. He would call. But Faith was not entirely sure what she was going to say to him when he did.

It might have been easier had Faith been able to more clearly define their relationship...or his motives. He was attracted to her, that much was obvious. He enjoyed being with her, or why else would he have sought her out twice in less than twenty-four hours? Of course he was attracted to her. Why else would a man send a woman thirty long-stemmed silver-pink roses?

Faith was an expert at reading the signs. She was accustomed to looking into a man's eyes and seeing desire there, or greed, or duplicity, or self-gratification. She knew all the smooth words and what they meant. She knew the body language behind them. She could sum up a man's character, motivations, needs and deficiencies in three seconds flat. A blink of the eye, a twitch of the finger, or a certain unconscious slant to the body could immediately alert Faith to danger signals the most studiously trained human behaviorist might have missed. She had learned the hard way, and she had never been fooled yet.

But no one had ever looked at her the way Ken Chapman did. No one had ever spoken to her the way he did. What did he see in her? What did he want? And how could she possibly be so confused by a man?

What was it Faith saw when she looked at him looking at her? She tried to be very logical about it. Whatever he wanted, it was in his eyes, in the expression of his face, in the very scent of the air that surrounded him...but she couldn't decipher it. For the first time in her life those well-honed senses that when translated to her brain could act like a computer printout of a man's psychological profile seemed to be failing her.

It wasn't sex. It was perhaps that which confused Faith the most. Oh, the attraction was there, the spark of chemistry, the subtle light of desire...she had seen it, she had felt it, she recognized it. But if she were completely honest she would have to admit that the spark was reciprocal, and perhaps what she was seeing in Ken's eyes was no more than a reflection of the attraction she felt for him. No, it was more than sex. When reflected in Ken Chapman's eyes, desire became transmuted into something deeper, more ethereal... and utterly baffling.

"So what's wrong with that?" she challenged Lancelot, who was giving her an utterly disgusted look as she nibbled at the last sausage link. "It's the nature of the species. Men and women are sometimes attracted to each other. Chemistry. The mating scent. I'm no different from anyone else."

That had a nice sound to it. For the past two years Faith had been trying to convince herself she was no different from anyone else. Maybe she was finally succeeding. Or maybe the healing and regeneration had been taking place subtly, so gradually she had not even noticed it, from the very first moment she had made the decision to leave Chicago.

Faith washed and put away the breakfast dishes thoughtfully, slowly coming to terms with this new idea. She was making it. She was recovering. It had been a long time now since she had conjured up the memory of Jess's face and felt anything but apathy. Now, when she tried, she was surprised to find she could hardly remember his face at all. Jess was the first man she had ever loved, and she had loved him with all her heart. Jess was also the first man ever to use her. And now Faith could barely remember what he looked like.

It was a good sign.

FAITH HAD NEVER considered herself a particularly striking woman. She was long-legged, skinny, with a delicate bone structure and rather plain features. But the
artist's eye of photographer Jess Warring had seen in
her a cross between the haute-couture qualities of fashion's most successful models and the elfin beauty of a
memorable cover girl. In her freshman year of college,
he had "discovered" her, he had groomed her, he had
introduced her to Margot Dreyser, owner of New
York's most prestigious modeling agency. He had given
Faith her start.

Faith dropped out of college to move to New York.
She lived with Jess Warring for almost a year, loved
him desperately, gave him all she had to give. She was
still uncertain about her new career, and despite Margot's best efforts, refused to commit herself to it fully.
Margot kept telling her she could be one of the biggest
names in the business, but fame did not appeal to Faith
and the business was a tawdry one. If there was a choice
between a fashion show in California and a weekend at
home with Jess, she chose Jess, without thinking twice.
That was where her commitment lay.

Unfortunately Jess did not feel the same way. He,
too, was pushing her toward advancement in her career, but Faith did not realize until much later that he
was more interested in the luxuries her extra income
could buy than in her personal success. She wanted to
please Jess; she started accepting more assignments.
She adopted the high-fashion image, complete with the

tinted hair that earned her the nickname "Copper." She let herself become more and more absorbed by the life-style, still intent upon only one thing—pleasing Jess.

When she was offered her first magazine cover, the only thing she thought about was how proud Jess would be. Faith left the agency as soon as she heard the news, bought a bottle of expensive wine, and came home to celebrate with Jess. He was in bed with another woman.

He told her calmly that he was sorry, and he had meant to tell her sooner, but this was the woman he was going to marry.

Jess left her with a nightmare of fury, rage and broken dreams, but that was all. When Faith came home from work the next afternoon, the apartment was cleaned out. So were their joint savings and checking accounts. Faith had worked for all of it in the time she had loved and lived with Jess; he had contributed little but promises. And in the end he took even that. Not being able to bear staying in New York, Faith moved to Chicago.

Faith remembered thinking at that time, on a high note of incredulous hysteria, *And I was raised to be such a good girl.* And perhaps that explained it all. She was raised to believe in love, in commitment, in sharing, in total devotion...and when a man like Jess had brought home the truth that those adjectives did not necessarily apply in the modern relationship, it hit her hard. It turned her around.

"Devastated" is too mild a word to describe what

Faith went through. She was too ashamed, and too broken, to admit her mistakes and go home to her parents. Work was her only salvation. Work, and fame and power and money...somehow achieving all that Jess had pushed her toward, and all that she had denied while she was living with him, enacted a twisted sort of revenge on him in her mind. She wanted to show him what he was missing. She wanted to show him how little she cared.

Before the year was out, Faith Hilliard was transformed from the simple Midwestern girl into Copper Adams, the most sought-after cover girl in the industry. Faith had been meek, shy, easily frightened, quick to lose control. Copper was beautiful, sophisticated and powerful. It was as simple as that.

Faith knew now all the reasons that had changed her life. Some of them were quite simple. It was easy. It was good money and a high life-style, glamour and adventure. It was comfortable to take the course of least resistance. Some reasons were more complicated. There was the feeling of power that came from people asking for her, wanting her, giving her the symbol of their own worth in the form of what was most important to them: money. There was vengeance at reclaiming what had been stolen from her—her innocence, her trust, as well as the symbol of her own worth. There was the complicated interplay of using and being used; the satisfaction of success. And there was the fantasy, for a time, of being someone she wasn't, doing things Faith Hilliard would never do, playing out a role and reaping the benefits.

She made obscene amounts of money and spent it just as obscenely. She traveled the world. She went to outrageous parties and movie premieres and the most publicized social events—always upon the arm of a different man. But none of those men ever got past her front door...until Gregory DeFrancis.

He was wealthy, powerful, charmingly Continental. He was also one of the most notorious underworld criminals of the decade.

Faith could justify to herself that she did not know who he was or what he did for a living until it was too late. And in fact no one, certainly not Gregory, ever spoke to her of it directly. But she must have known. The bodyguards, the bulletproof limousines, the terse late-night telephone conversations...she would have been a fool not to have known.

She liked Gregory. He was amusing, cynically self-effacing, surprisingly tender. They were friends as well as, for a brief time, lovers. And Faith was in his Chicago penthouse when the FBI came that night to take him away.

She had known Gregory for three months, and in that time, by actual count, they had spent less than fifteen days together. But the presence of the glamorous Copper Adams in the apartment of Gregory DeFrancis at the time of his arrest put her at the volcanic center of an already sensational case. The tabloids had a field day. Even respectable papers could not refer to the De-Francis case without mentioning "Cover Girl Copper Adams," and magazines that once had paid exorbitant fees for her photograph now did feature articles on her—for free. Faith was even subpoenaed in the case, but federal officers soon learned she could tell them nothing they did not already know, and her testimony was not needed.

She saw Gregory once before he was sentenced. There was not enough history between them to warrant much soul-searching conversation...only enough history to change her life. So they chatted in an easy, desultory fashion, Gregory no different from his usual charmingly cynical, wryly matter-of-fact self, and not the least worried about the ten years in federal prison awaiting him—of which he might serve two. Just before Faith left, Gregory winked at her, and in his best James Cagney imitation said, "That's life in the fast lane, sweetheart." Faith smiled and left and never saw Gregory or anyone associated with him again.

Going to visit Gregory was just the final period to a decision Faith had made long ago, a realization that had not crept up on her suddenly, but had hit her over the head like a sledgehammer. It was over. The fantasy of flashing lights and hot colors had faded into the stark realism of self-destruction, and Faith had to come face-to-face with who and what she was. She did not like what she saw.

Within a week she had packed her car with what little she wanted to save of her former life, and was taking the interstate out of Chicago. The quiet charm of Little Creek, Indiana, called out to her, and she stopped.

Sometimes she still reflected distantly on how easy it all was to leave behind. No one who knew her now would associate Faith Hilliard with the notorious Copper Adams, nor did she particularly want to remind them. Without the dramatic makeup, the glamorous clothes, the bimonthly hair rinse—the formula for which had been a trade secret—she was just another woman on the streets. Faith Hilliard, florist in a small town, model citizen, a little too skinny, rather plain in appearance, minding her own business and keeping mostly to herself. She liked it that way.

And she rarely, if ever, looked back.

THE DAY WAS BALMY and filled with the sounds and scents and colors of spring. Faith took her gardening tools and went outside, leaving the windows and doors open to air the house—and also so that she would be sure to hear the telephone or the doorbell if it rang. Turning the cool, moist soil in her hands, tugging tender weeds from the earth, feeling the sun on her hair and inhaling the scents of growing things was a self-hypnotic therapy for Faith; she let her thoughts take her where they would.

Faith knew men too well to be enchanted with them anymore. Her years at the top had brought her into contact with the best and the worst of them, and little surprised her now. There was no illusion left, and without the element of fantasy, romance was an empty shell. The man-woman interaction could be neatly summed up in a phrase: the need to use and be used. Men were just as afraid of women as women were of men, just as afraid of rejection and loneliness; so much so that they would pay for companionship to avoid it. To say Faith had no respect for men would be an untruth. She had respect for all living things, and under-standing only generated compassion within her. But until now she had no need for a relationship, or any hope of one. The value of that commodity had been greatly diminished by the cheapness with which it had been regarded in the world of Copper Adams.

But she wasn't talking about a lifetime commitment here. She wasn't necessarily even talking about a love affair, or a sexual encounter. Faith did not know whether she was strong enough to handle that yet. But a relationship, a friendship, a little touch of ro-mance...

"For goodness' sake," she grumbled to Lancelot, who was industriously tilling the soil in her tulip bed and then rolling in it with a decadent pleasure that would have made his forebears proud, "I don't even know anyone in this town but you. And I came here to start a new life, didn't I? To be a new person. Give me one good reason why that new life shouldn't include a man. I'm not the same person anymore."

Faith was aware of the reputation Copper Adams had built—a reputation that practically sizzled after the inci-dent with Gregory DeFrancis. Some of it was deserved, and for that she was ashamed; most of it was not, but she still struggled with guilt. She wasn't very proud of the person Copper Adams had been, or of the self-serving, pleasure-seeking life she had led. Perhaps she was not exactly the gun moll the papers had made her out to be, but she was no angel in white, either. She was sorry for that, and for the reckless and confused impulses that had led her into a frenetic life that would eventually culminate in the bed of a high-powered criminal. But there was nothing she could do to change it. She had learned to acknowledge the past, accept it and put it behind her.

Faith refused to punish herself for things that could not be changed. She merely lived with them.

And she was a different person now.

It was a realization that took some getting used to. Who was this new Faith Hilliard and what did she want? The last time she had asked herself that—the only time she could recall ever asking herself what she really wanted—her answer had been this: a small town where no one knew her, a little house and a shop of her own, flowers. The beauty and perfume of nature to cleanse her soiled soul. Peace. Silence. Solitude. But time had passed since then, changes she had hardly even been aware of had taken place, and suddenly a man with gray-rimmed eyes walked into her life, and Faith Hilliard found herself asking whether she dared reach for more.

"It scares me, Lance," she whispered, kneeling in the soft soil with her spade resting limply in her hand. But the cat was nowhere to be found.

At three o'clock in the afternoon Ken still had not called. Faith was both puzzled and more disturbed than she liked to admit. Could she have misjudged him? Maybe he was doing nothing more than engaging in a mild flirtation with her.

Did a man spend ninety-three dollars and ninety-six cents on a flirtation?

Maybe his interest in her, whatever it was, had been

satisfied by the long day spent with her yesterday. Maybe he was the type of person who collected character studies the way other people collected stamps. Maybe he was bored, and, Faith had to admit, not without good reason. Maybe he had decided she simply wasn't worth the trouble.

"Maybe," she suggested to Lance with a weak, slightly rueful smile, "I'm slipping."

Faith curled up on the divan before the open window with a paperback book, deciding that since this Sunday was apparently going to be no different from any other, she may as well spend it as she did every other. The air drifting over her was fresh and spring-scented, the sky a lazy study in pastel blue and confectioner's clouds. The distant sound of children at play reached her, the occasional lazy footsteps of a couple on an afternoon walk. It was a perfect day for anything—a picnic, a softball game, a walk—anything that was done in groups of two or more. *I would have gone with him today,* Faith finally admitted to herself, *anywhere. If he had asked me.*

Eventually she dozed and drifted off to sleep in the sunlight. Neither the telephone nor the doorbell disturbed her.

At five-thirty, soporific and hazy from her nap, Faith wandered into the kitchen to make a cup of tea. Then, as was her custom on Sunday afternoons, she called her mother.

"I can set my watch by you," Faith's mother greeted her cheerfully on the second ring. "How are you, baby?"

The worst of it all was what the notoriety of the De-Francis scandal had done to Faith's parents. Their middle-class morals had been hard put to accept the life-style of their cover-girl daughter, but limitless in their love, they had somehow found a way to do so—and even to be proud of her success. When the De-Francis case had erupted, Faith's worst nightmares were about what her parents must be suffering, but through it all they had expressed nothing but concern for her. They had never doubted their daughter's goodness and innocence, not once. That their trust was so fully undeserved was one thing Faith would never completely forgive herself for.

But never again would she put that trust in jeopardy.

Faith settled back in the armchair, cuddling the telephone receiver in one hand and the teacup in the other. "I'm great," she told her, a standard reply whether or not it was true. "How's Dad? Did you get the transmission fixed on the station wagon?"

They chatted for a few minutes about the happenings and lack of the same since Faith's last phone call a week ago to the minute. Her father was still arguing with the mechanic over the repair bill, her mother had given a talk at her garden club only to return home and find her peonies were dying of some strange disease. They discussed possible causes and cures for a time, and Faith told her mother about the wedding and the disasters that had ensued, making it all sound so slapstick that her mother was gasping with laughter by the time she finished. Faith did not mention Ken Chapman.

They talked about the weather and relatives, and for fifteen minutes Faith was transported back to the house in which she had grown up, the homey smells and gentle colors, chatty neighbors and small-time troubles. For fifteen minutes she felt loved and welcome, the only daughter of parents who thought she was as close to perfect as it was possible for a human being to be. Perfect she may not be, but Faith was on her way. Now.

When she hung up, Faith was nostalgically happy, content in a vaguely homesick way. She made what was, for her, an elaborate dinner of frozen scallops and sautéed vegetables, and shared it with Lancelot. And at seven o'clock she still had not heard from Ken.

Faith had no right to be hurt or offended, and she wasn't. She was merely bewildered. Faith knew men. She knew their weaknesses and their needs, their demands and their games. She knew their secret fantasies, their fears, their hopes and their fragilities. She had made a life out of reading their signals and responding to them in front of a camera. It disturbed her to suspect that perhaps this time she had read wrong.

But Ken was not like any man she had ever met. He had looked at her and he had seen her weaknesses, her fears, her secrets. She had never caught a glimpse of his, and it made her uneasy to think that that was perhaps because he had none.

He sent her flowers. Faith smiled a little to herself as she stroked the blossoming rosebud that was the single ornament on her dining table, remembering how it had felt against her skin, remembering how he had looked at her. What was it he had said? She frowned a little, trying to remember. It sounded like poetry, but something about it reminded her of the little girl in a starched dress and black patent leathers, sitting in Sunday school. Her face softened as it came drifting back to her. Faith, the substance of things hoped for... it was her name. The substance of things hoped for. A single pink rose... for hope. No, Ken Chapman was not like anyone she had ever known.

He was the only man, she realized slowly, who had looked at her and seemed to be wondering what he could give her, not what he could take.

And she knew she wanted to see him again.

At eight o'clock, Faith went down to the shop. The purpose of her mission, she told herself, was to check on the cooler, which was running admirably. But at eight-thirty she added a second pink rosebud to the bloom in the vase on her table. After all, she reasoned, he had paid for them.

When Faith went to bed at ten o'clock, Ken still had not called. And Faith was still hoping that he would.

Chapter Six

The cooler was still chugging away when Faith opened the shop the next morning. She turned off the alarm, turned on the lights, plugged in the coffeepot, and checked the flowers in the cooler one more time, just to make sure. They were as fresh as when she and Ken had placed them there Saturday night. Then, self-consciously and almost surreptitiously, she took the small portable radio she had brought from home and plugged it in near the potted plants, tuning it to a low-volume classical station. It didn't hurt to try, she supposed.

Sally was almost on time. It was enough of a good sign to discourage Faith from continuing the notice-of-termination-of-employment speech Ken had interrupted Saturday, and besides, it turned out to be a busy morning. The repairmen came, grumbling vociferously over the patch job that had saved Faith's flowers over the weekend, took three hours to make it permanent, and presented her with a bill that actually made Faith's stomach turn. Sally was kept busy with deliveries all morning and the telephone all afternoon while Faith put together arrangements in the back room. Every time the doorbell announced a customer, Faith peeked out into the front room, but it was never the person she was looking for.

A few minutes before four Faith told Sally to close up for her—"Not a minute before five-thirty," she warned sternly and ran across the street to the bank. The pretty cumulus clouds of the day before had lowered and grayed and begun to sprinkle the famed April showers, and Faith could not remember whether Lancelot had been in or out that morning. He would be in a sulk for days if he had to wait in the rain for Faith to come home.

"Need to get that stupid cat his own key," she muttered to herself as she came out of the bank, pausing for a moment to take her rain scarf out of her coat pocket.

"I beg your pardon?" said Ken Chapman at her elbow.

Faith whirled, and it was more pleasure than surprise that lit her eyes. He registered it with a reciprocal spark in his. "Hello!" she said, and if her voice sounded a little breathless, there was nothing she could do about it. He had startled her, that was all.

He was wearing a brown sports jacket and a pale peach-colored shirt with the top two buttons open. The tie that had once completed the outfit was poking its edges out of his jacket pocket. A fine mist of rain had congealed in sparkles on his hair, and his eyes were almost the color of a tropical forest. He was smiling at her.

"You're all dressed up today," Faith commented, simply because she could not think of anything better to say. The rain had lightened, and she tucked her scarf back into her pocket. Or was it feminine vanity that made her not want to be seen by him in a plastic cap with tacky gold spangles splashed all over it?

He nodded and touched her arm as the light changed for them to cross. "I've been to the hospital," he answered. Then, registering the quick alarm on her face, he laughed. "Just visiting," he assured her.

She wondered if someone close to him was ill and if that could explain where he had been all day yesterday, but it seemed inappropriate to offer sympathy or ask questions when he offered no indication of concern, so Faith said, "The cooler held. The repairmen were very upset."

Again he chuckled. "The pride of the American working man is a very noble thing. Did they make rubble of my efforts and do the job right?"

Faith nodded. "At the cost of half my year's profits." They were standing in front of Faith's shop, and she placed her hand on the door handle of the van.

Ken lifted an eyebrow. "Going home early?"

"That's what I have an assistant for," she told him, and then grimaced. "Or at least that's what I'm supposed to have an assistant for. I have to take advantage of the days she actually shows up and leave when I can."

Ken looked at her pointedly. "Aren't you forgetting something?"

It took less than a second to understand, and with a

look of totally feigned dry resignation, she went back inside·and retrieved a pink rose.

The mist had slackened to a momentary lull, and Ken was still waiting for her when she returned, looking thoughtfully up at the white-shingle sign that hung over her doorway. "I feel silly," she told him as she opened the van door and placed the rose, carefully wrapped in tissue paper, on the passenger seat. She did not mention that she had not forgotten yesterday.

"Do you know," Ken said reflectively, turning away from his survey of her quaint, antique-red storefront, "I've passed this place many times, and I always stopped, or looked twice." He smiled, but he seemed to be perfectly serious. "There always seemed to be something special about it. It drew me. Maybe it was just because it was such an eye-catching little spot, with the potted flowers in the window boxes in the spring and the Christmas decorations in the winter...it was charming, like something out of another century." Faith warmed to his elaborate praise, but·a tingle started in her stomach as he added with a special smile, "Maybe it was intuition. I even went inside once," he said,·and before she had a chance to react to that last comment, added, "but you weren't there."

"Did you buy anything?" Faith inquired brightly, stepping up into the van. But she, too, was thinking about life's strange coincidences, and where they would be now if they had met earlier, and how peculiar it was that he had been walking these same streets, driving these same roads, looking inside her shop all this time and neither had known the other·existed until now. It was a fanciful train of thought that Faith tried to dismiss impatiently. There were hundreds of people she had never met in this town who passed her shop every day; he was only one of them. Ken simply had a way of making everything sound romantic and enchanted, and Faith was falling for it again....

He answered, "Not a thing. I didn't have anyone I wanted to send roses to at the time."

She placed her hand on the key, looking down at him. The moment seemed to be fraught with anticipation, but Ken was simply smiling up at her with friendly ease, and what now? A five-minute conversation after an accidental meeting at the bank and another "see you around"? Her mind was twisted into knots, trying to figure him out. Maybe she had been wrong about him. Maybe she didn't need the hassle. Wasn't he going to say anything...?

Faith turned the ignition key, intending to let the engine warm up for a while. That would give him a chance, she reasoned, to prolong this encounter if he wished, while also indicating that she did not intend to hang around all day in the van waiting for him to ask her out. But when she twisted the key, nothing happened. She tried again and got nothing but the mechanical click of the key in the lock. She stared incredulously at the steering wheel. "I don't believe this!" she exclaimed softly, turning the key again, with more force this time. "I just had a new battery installed Saturday!"

"Has it been driven today?" Ken inquired.

Faith turned the key several more times, furiously

and ineffectually. "I drove it all day yesterday, and Sally's been out making deliveries today—" Sally. She had obviously done something to wreck the engine—and then Faith was ashamed of herself. There was no call to heap all her troubles on the hapless girl's head, and it went beyond the bounds of logic to accuse her of sabotaging the van.

She looked down at Ken, and a slow, beautiful grin spread over his face. "See what happens when you believe in miracles?" he said, extending his hand to her. "I get to drive you home."

Faith had the most uncanny impression that he had known this was going to happen, that he was waiting for it, confident and unconcerned. What was it he had said about the unseen hand?

Of course there was a multitude of other solutions. It was only a little after four; she could have called the garage and had them send someone out immediately. She could have gotten a ride from Sally. She could even have looked under the hood herself, or Ken could have, and found what was no doubt a perfectly minor and easily repairable source of the trouble. But after only a second's hesitation, Faith picked up the rose and her purse and climbed out of the van. Ken kept his hand lightly on her back as they crossed the street to where his car was parked.

Ken drove a five-year-old Torino whose interior smelled comfortably of old books and road dust. It had been a long time since Faith had been in a man's car. A very long time.

It started sprinkling again as they were under way,

turning the passing landscape into a runny watercolor of spring greens and yellows between the squish and swipe of the windshield wipers. It was warm inside the car, and the patter of the rain, the hum of the engine and the rhythm of the wipers created a cozy intimacy that Faith was not quite sure how to react to. She wanted to relax and enjoy it, but she couldn't.

"Pick one," Ken said, signaling the turn that would lead them out of town. "You are: a) nervous, b) uncomfortable, c) ready to jump out of the car at the next stoplight."

Faith choked on a startled laugh, turning to look out the misty window. She saw nothing but the pattern of raindrops tugged against the glass by the wind. "How about d?" she decided. "None of the above."

"Liar," he chided gently, and the glance Faith met in quick defense was both sympathetic and mildly teasing. She said nothing, but concentrated on the friendly squeak of the windshield wipers, trying to look relaxed.

"I've been trying to figure out since Saturday what it is I do that makes you so nervous," Ken continued conversationally. "Is it my overpowering charm? My devastating good looks? My incredible virility? Don't laugh," he objected, affecting injury. "I'll have you know that in my senior year of college I had a team of paramedics follow me around just to resuscitate the women that were swooning at my feet—self-defense against lawsuits, you know."

Faith glanced at him, eyes sparkling with repressed giggles. "If you came on as strong to them as you did to me, I can see why."

"Notice, however," he pointed out, lifting a finger, "that I've made a great effort to tone it down today. No extravagant gestures, no dramatic declarations, no flamboyant entrances and exits... all at great expense to my self-control, I might add. Are you impressed?"

"Greatly," Faith agreed, eyes still twinkling. "You strike me as the type of person who could use a little self-control."

Again he pulled an injured face. "Undisciplined? Me? Never!" Then, in mock demand, "Are you implying that you prefer the subtle approach to the hard sell of my overpowering personality?"

Faith looked him over once, up and down, lips tightening with laughter, eyes glittering with speculative mirth. "Maybe a little bit of both," she decided.

Ken glanced at her, and the softening of his eyes played dangerously with her sense of balance. "Good," he said simply. "I wouldn't like to think you didn't want me to approach you at all."

They had reached her house, and Ken pulled into the driveway, close to the front door. Faith saw a shadow leap to the window in the quick flash of his headlights, and felt a minor relief that she would not have to contend with a soggy and disgruntled cat that evening. She paused with her hand on the door handle, turning to thank him and wondering whether or not to invite him in, but he saved her the trouble.

"I'll bet," Ken announced with sudden decision, switching off the ignition, "that you're the type of girl who likes to walk in the rain."

Faith did not have a chance to question or protest,

for he was already out of the car and opening her door. "Do you mean—now?" she demanded, half-laughing, as he extended his hand for her.

"A moment wasted is a moment lost," he philoso-phized cheerfully. "Who knows when we'll get such perfect rain for walking again?"

Faith looked at him for a moment, but she really didn't think about it twice. She burst into laughter and put her hand in his.

Faith walked in the rain when she was upset, or feeling lonely or confined or restless; sometimes she did it just to feel the dew on her face and taste the clean fresh scents of earth opening and flowers blos-soming. The rain that afternoon was sweet-smelling, warm, a gentle haze that clung rather than fell, tick-ling her skin and caressing her hair. There was an in-timacy about their echoing footsteps on the empty, fresh-washed streets, a magic to the early dusk that misted lime-green lawns and pastel flower beds. Ken's hand was warm on hers, large and firm. The feel of it, the presence of him in easy step beside her, seemed to color the world with a subtle rosy glow. She had not felt this good, this simple and carefree and content, since she was a child.

"When I was a kid," she said, smiling with delight at the memory, "my mom would let me put on my swim-suit and play in the rain. I'd splash in the mud puddles and sail boats in the gutters and slide down grassy banks—and even though we had a neighborhood pool less than a block away, I never had as much fun there as I did just playing in the rain." She tilted her head back to better catch the droplets on her face. "I wonder why that is."

"When I was a kid," Ken answered, "I used to sit up in a tree after a storm and wait for the little girls to come by. And when they walked underneath I'd do this." He reached up deftly and grabbed the low-hanging branch of a blossoming apple tree, shaking it violently, splattering water and apple blossoms everywhere.

Faith squealed at the dousing and jumped away. Apple blossoms caught in her hair, and raindrops glittered on her lashes. "I should have figured," she sputtered, brushing at the splotches on her coat. "I'll bet you were the type of boy who put wormy apples on the teacher's desk, too."

"Nuh-uh." Ken's eyes were dancing as he reached up to remove a single blossom from her hair. But he left most of them there, because they looked so pretty entwined with the multicolored golds and blonds and browns of her hair—ethereal, fairylike, almost mythological. She was a Greek goddess in harmony with her elements. "I put snakes in their drawers."

She lifted an eyebrow. "Desk drawers, I presume."

Ken widened his eyes innocently, but could not disguise the laughing spark of mischief there. "But of course."

Faith gave a toss to her damp, flower-gloried hair, and then they both broke into laughter.

Ken draped his arm around her shoulders as they started walking again. The soft rain grew denser, bending the heavy heads of daffodils and bouncing off waxy tulips, making a musical swishing sound on the side-walk. Faith carried the rose, and the tissue paper grew soggy in her hand as pearly beads of moisture con-densed on the silken surface and rolled off. They were silent, absorbing the rain and the gentle twilight with the same quiet welcome as did the earth around them, drawing it in and letting it become part of them. It felt natural to be moving with Ken, the weight of his arm around Faith's shoulders, his body close to hers. His scent, as clean and as natural as the rain around them but subtly different, mingled with that of growing grass and blossoming hyacinths and the heady sweetness of the rose as she brought it to her face, and the combina-tion was warmly intoxicating.

"You're awfully quiet," Faith commented after a while.

"I'm practicing subtlety," he assured her.

Faith smiled, inhaling the fragrance of the rose again. "Why did you send the roses?" she asked unex-pectedly, after a few more footsteps.

Ken did not hesitate in his reply. "So you would think of me, at least once a day, every day, for the next month, guaranteed."

Faith wanted to ask why he wanted her to think of him, and what he wanted her to think about him, and why he had gone to so much trouble to guarantee such attention from a total stranger...but such questions seemed inappropriate in the mystical fairy-tale world in which they walked so companionably. It was enough, right now, to let it be.

The rain steadily increased as they circled the block

and headed back toward Faith's house, but they did not increase their pace. Light was slowly fading into a lavender netherworld sealed by a curtain of silvery rain, and nothing existed except the splash of droplets against leaves and the whisper of trickling gutters and the eerie echo of their footsteps on the sidewalk. It was spooky, in an enchanted way, a deserted planet, an empty landscape, a magical time warp charged with possibilities.

Sharing her thoughts, Ken began to hum the theme to "The Twilight Zone" beneath his breath. Faith giggled as he announced, deepening his voice to an eerie monotone, "A man and a woman out for a walk in a familiar neighborhood. Neighbors are safe inside their doors, watching television, eating dinner. Home is only half a block away. Little do they know that the next step they take will move them out of the world of their own suburban neighborhood and into the realm of... the Twilight Zone."

He gave a low, wicked chuckle that began deep in his throat and escalated to a crazed pitch, and Faith squealed and slapped at him playfully, laughing. "Stop that! I can do without the sound effects!"

His eyes snapping wickedly, he went on in his malevolent stage voice, "It hides in the bushes, it snakes through the fog, it creeps up behind them..."

She broke away from him, laughter dancing in her eyes, walking backward before him. "You're a very weird person, Ken Chapman!"

"Its hot breath parts the fog, its yellow eyes glow..." He raised his hands into threatening hooked claws. "A sound, a movement, it leaps...." He snatched at her and Faith squealed, breaking into a run.

Gasping and laughing like children, they reached Faith's doorstep half a minute after the gentle rain had turned into a drenching downpour. Ken, without a raincoat, had no doubt taken the worst of it, and Faith turned to make some scolding remark to him about poetic justice when her breath stopped as he caught her face in his hands. She had just a moment to see the light and laughter in his gray-green eyes, the raindrops clinging to his skin and dripping from his hair, and then he was kissing her.

He caught her off-guard. She didn't expect it. Had she had even a second's warning, the defenses would have been up, for at the first sign of his intimate touch the real Faith would have gone into hiding and the automaton that took her place on such occasions would have sprung into place, making the appropriate sounds and gestures, doing what was expected of her, giving the proper response, feeling nothing. But she had no warning, and in an instant Ken had captured the essence of Faith between his hands and was penetrating it slowly, beautifully, opening it and exploring it with wonder and delight, and Faith was helpless to do anything but let it happen.

His skin was cool, his lips soft. He was drinking of her, delicately, exquisitely, tasting the rain on her skin and the flavor of her natural perfume, drawing from her, giving to her. His tongue flickered over her lips, his mouth brushing hers, his breath flowing into her. Clasping, releasing, gentle nibbling kisses and butterfly sweeps of the tongue that acted on Faith's senses like a drug, a powerful euphoriant that carried her up and left her suspended in midair, anchored only by the touch of Ken's hands and the caress of his lips. His fingers gathered raindrops on her skin in delicate caresses that his lips followed, pushing back her hair, tilting her head to receive the warm tasting of his tongue and his lips. There was no urgency, no demand, Ken was simply kissing her, reveling in her, delighting in her. And Faith was floating with it, captured in it, melting into it.

Faith did not recognize the responses of her own body anymore. She did not know when the muscles of her knees weakened and she swayed against him or when the hand that still held the rose came up and curled against his neck. There was a weightless sensation in the pit of her stomach, a giddy flow of ether through her veins, and all of her—all of her—seemed to be opening up to him, unfolding petal by petal beneath the gentle provocative coaxing of his lips. Her face was pliant in his hands, responding to each touch, yearning toward each stroke of thumb or fingers or tongue. She had never imagined being kissed like this. It was not a reciprocal action, nothing was demanded of her. It was light, it was delicate, it was sweet, it was absorbing. It was the quick flicker of repetitive pleasure that blinded like lightning, the worshipful unfolding of sensual delight that lingered and transported; it enfolded all of her.

He tasted her, he worshiped her, he could not get enough of her. He licked the raindrops off her face and feathered her eyelashes with kisses. His breath was warm, breezing over her face. His fingers were strong, cupped against her forehead. His lips were soft. His cheek was rough but slippery as he rubbed it against hers, the tip of his nose cold. She felt the tickling flutter of wet lashes on her temple, the silken smooth arch of an eyebrow. And when he lifted his face from hers, slowly, with lingering butterfly kisses, it took Faith a long, dazed moment to realize what had happened.

Her consciousness slowly coalesced into the sound of rain rushing through the gutters and warm night closing rapidly around them, a firm and solid porch beneath her feet, a metal awning over her head, her own front door inches away. Ken was still holding her face, and the light in his eyes was so deep, the smile on his face so gentle, so delighted and pleasure-hazed, that it was impossible to feel any of the confusion or apprehension or even shock that should have accompanied the moment. It was impossible to do anything but share the moment, to return his smile, though somewhat tremulously, and to let the natural goodness in his eyes penetrate her, caress and soothe her, and make her feel right.

Ken smoothed a damp wisp of hair behind her ear; he dropped his hands. Faith turned and fumbled for her key, at last finding it. Her fingers were clumsy, overheated and a little disconnected, as though all the feeling had not quite returned to them yet, as though part of her was still floating high up in the stratosphere with Ken as her guide. She was glad when Ken took the key from her and opened the door.

Ken noticed a little sign above the doorbell that he had missed the last time he was there. In tiny Gothic script it said Beware of Attack Cat. His smile deepened as he returned Faith's key to her, and there was no reticence in her manner as she gestured him inside. That, more than anything else, made him happy. She was beginning to relax with him.

"Your jacket is wet," Faith noticed as she turned on the lamp and shrugged out of her own raincoat. "If you'll take it off, I...can hang it up in the bathroom and it won't take too long to dry." Now that he was actually inside, she was beginning to feel a little bit nervous, and the words came out awkwardly. She did not know why she had invited him inside...except that it had seemed so natural. Except that she wanted to spend more time with him. Except that she was still in a half-floating daze of euphoria and she hadn't thought about it at all. It felt strange to have him here, where no man had been before.

He obligingly shrugged out of his jacket and handed it to her, his alert, perceptive eyes busy meanwhile going over the room, examining and analyzing with appreciation and sensitivity. Faith was not sorry she had asked him in.

"I'll be just a minute," she called over her shoulder as she went into the kitchen to put the rose in water. "Have a seat."

The silver-pink rain-drenched rose joined two others on the dining-room table, and when Faith crossed back through the living room, Ken was smiling as he examined a whimsical collection of painted tiles over the desk that served as her bar. Faith slipped silently into her bedroom.

She hung Ken's jacket carefully on a clothes hanger from the shower rod, turned on the space heater, and closed the bathroom door. She exchanged her soggy shoes for a pair of fuzzy bedroom slippers, and realized in the nick of time that they looked ridiculous with the short flowered caftan she was wearing. She took them off. She rubbed her damp hair with a towel and smiled when she discovered a few apple blossoms entangled there, then brushed it loose around her shoulders. She found another towel for Ken and came back into the living room, barefoot.

At the threshold she stopped. Ken was sitting on the sofa, and upon his knees, sleepy-eyed and content, reposed Lancelot. Not only was the generally antisocial cat allowing his ears to be scratched—and apparently enjoying every minute—but he was actually purring, loudly enough to be heard across the room. Faith blinked once, speechless with amazement, and crossed the room toward them. She stood directly in front of Ken, staring down at the curious phenomenon studiously, and Ken glanced up at her.

"He likes me," Ken explained, quite unnecessarily.

"Incredible," Faith murmured.

"Oh, I don't know," protested Ken mildly, and Lancelot tilted his head to the gentle scratching motions of Ken's fingers. "A lot of people like me."

"That 'attack cat' sign is not entirely a joke," Faith told him. "I've never known him to do anything but hiss and spit at strangers. He's actually bitten one or two. What did you do, hypnotize him?"

Ken glanced up at her, that sweet, ineffable grin

spreading across his features and tugging at Faith's heart. "I'll never tell."

Charmer, Faith thought dazedly. That's what he is, a certified charmer, and he's hypnotized us both. . . .

She shook herself out of the silly reverie and remembered the business at hand. "I brought you a towel," she said. She could not help noticing that his shirt and his dark pants were also splotched with water. His feet were probably wet, too. But she was not going to ask this man to undress in her house and sit cozily wrapped in a blanket or a towel while she dried his clothes. There were limits to her hospitality . . . and to the risks she was willing to take. "Do you want a grilled-cheese sandwich?" she offered, and then realized she had done it. She had invited him to stay for dinner.

"Sounds great." He accepted the towel from her, and ran it once across his glistening hair. As he lifted his arms, the wet parts of his shirt clung to his skin, outlining his torso. "I'll help."

Carefully depositing Lancelot on the sofa, Ken draped the towel around his neck and followed her into the kitchen. Lancelot, scowling after them for a moment in evident resentment, eventually jumped down from the sofa and padded behind them.

Ken smiled when he saw the three roses in the bud vase, appreciated the unusual details of her kitchen—the lithographs and 1930s comic strips that Faith had found in the attic and framed, the fern stand made of what someone had told her was part of a threshing machine she had found in the underbrush in back of the house—and the awkwardness Faith had expected to experience working side by side with a man at her own stove simply disappeared. Ken fried bacon as Faith chopped cheese, and when the bacon was done he crumbled it over the inside of the sandwiches that were ready to be grilled. He told her about his childhood in Michigan and his one-time dreams of fame as a pro hockey player, and they laughed together as Lancelot ran off with a strip of bacon when they weren't looking.

"I'll drive you to work in the morning," Ken volunteered when, by mutual agreement, they had decided to let the villain keep his spoils and turned back to the stove. "I'll take a look at the van, too. It's probably just a loose battery cable—that sometimes happens when you have a new battery installed."

Faith stared at him. "Well, if you knew that was it, why didn't you fix it this afternoon?"

His eyes twinkled. "And miss all this? Are you kidding?"

Faith felt an absurdly delightful blush creep out of her collar, and she turned busily to open a cabinet.

Faith heated a can of vegetable soup and Ken made hot chocolate, and they took their plates into the living room, sitting on the floor at the coffee table while reruns of "Star Trek" flickered on the television set before them. It was an evening at home enhanced by the company of someone special, and Faith had never imagined she could enjoy anything so much.

When Faith turned the television set off they settled back on the sofa in the warm glow of a single lamp, sipping hot chocolate and talking in an easy, desultory fashion. Faith curled her bare feet under her skirt and watched the play of lamplight in her chocolate, amazed at how relaxed she was, and how content. Nothing about her haphazard, whimsically furnished home would ever look the same now that he had been a part of it. She did not need the steadily growing vase of roses to remind her of him every day. He was here, an integral part of her and all that was around her, and when he left there would be an emptiness.

That realization startled Faith, and disturbed her. Already Ken had insinuated himself into her life—there was no point in denying it—but how had it happened? How had she let it happen? Surely she had not intended to. She hadn't even intended to allow his physical presence to become a distraction on the outskirts of her life, but somehow he was beginning to entwine himself around her emotions, and that was infinitely more dangerous.

Silence had fallen, but it was such an easy, comfortable one that Faith did not even notice until Ken spoke into it. "So," he said gently, "what do you think?"

Their empty cups had been placed on the table before them long ago, and Ken was sitting with his arm stretched out along the sofa cushions behind her. He was sitting close enough for Faith to feel his warmth, and she had not noticed that before, either. The rain had slowed to a mere sprinkle again; it whispered like silk against the rafters and gleamed like jewels on the windowpane. Lance, replete with their leftovers and disdaining the nasty weather outside, had settled on a chair opposite them, his front paws tucked under his chest and his yellow eyes watching them unblinkingly.

Faith glanced up at Ken. "About what?"

Ken's eyes, so kind, so soft, so infinitely absorbing, fell upon Faith like a caress. His smile barely touched his lips, but softened his whole face. "About me," he answered, and his thumb and forefinger absently captured Faith's earlobe, stroking lightly. She shivered. "Us, the future, life in general..."

For just another moment Faith's eyes were caught by the thoughtful demand in his, and then she broke away. What did she think? What indeed? That this was the gentlest, kindest, most captivating man she had ever met, that his very presence seemed to weave some sort of shimmering web around her whose strands were impossible to break? That his touch incited her to mindless pleasure, that his smile did something potentially dangerous to her heart and that she could look into those strange green eyes forever? That he was confusing, exasperating, titillating and totally mind-bending, and that each moment spent with him was a new experience in excitement, discovery and uncertainty? That if he left right now and was never seen or heard from again her life would be forever touched by his brief presence in it... that he scared her.

Faith bent forward quickly, away from that electrifying touch of his fingertips on her ear, and reached for their cups. "Would you like some more cocoa?"

"No." There could have been a touch of gentle amusement in Ken's voice, and the light pressure of his hand on her shoulder brought Faith back to him again. His eyes were alight with sweetness and desire. "What I would like is this."

In a single smooth and graceful movement he turned her into his arms and covered her mouth gently with his. Gently it began, a soft reassurance of the comforting nature of the man who held her, but the kiss slowly and irretrievably built into the hazy swirling of passion that was inevitable, that was meant to be. There was no tentativeness now, no sweet exploration, no playful discovery. This was the kiss a man gave to a woman, deep and overpowering and sense-filling, demanding and drawing and fulfilling. And again it captured Faith. She wanted to pull away, emotionally and mentally if not physically, to accept his kiss and be unaffected, to respond to it as he expected her to but to be untouched. It was impossible to be anywhere near the scope of this man's vibrance and be untouched. His mouth took unhesitant possession of hers, his tongue a sweet and swift invasion, and Faith melted into it.

Her pulses injected a rush of sense-enhancing, mind-numbing adrenaline through her veins, her breath narrowed into a shallow stream, patches of heat sprang up on her body and gradually began to merge into a single sheet of tingling, stinging warmth. Ken's fingers were strong and supple on her waist and the small of her back; the other hand gently entwined itself in her hair. Faith could feel the dampness of his shirt against the palm of her hand where she had braced against his chest, preparing to push away, and beneath it the heat of his skin. But she didn't push away. For her other hand was on his waist, her fingers, with a mind of their own, were caressing the taut, spare flesh there, and then the hand that had been pressing his chest slipped

upward to his shoulder, exploring the warm smooth-
ness of the back of his neck, slipping beneath his collar,
and she was drinking of him as he was of her, absorbing
him and opening herself up to him.

Her face turned to the motion as his mouth slipped
from hers and brushed a delicate path across her chin
and upward to her cheek, little trails of fire igniting
with the whisper of his breath across her oversensitized
skin. His tongue flickered around her ear and a shiver
tingled down her spine as he explored the delicate crev-
ice between lobe and neck.

A slow, exquisite and paralyzing weakness spread
downward from the darting pressure of his tongue
against the hollow formed by the curve of her collarbone, and she was helpless against the response of her
own body. She was helpless against the breathlessness,
the heaviness of her limbs, the tingling pleasure and
tightening need that shut down her reasoning and admitted nothing but the sensation of him. She was helpless against the thundering of her heart that only gained
momentum as his hand moved slowly downward, tracing the curve of her hip and the shape of her leg beneath the curtain of her skirt, finding at last her bare
foot nestled on the sofa and caressing it. Her breath
stopped entirely with the curiously erotic massaging
motions of his fingers against her toes and instep, waiting for his hand to move higher, discovering her ankle
and following the curve of her leg upward again, beneath the skirt this time....

Her lips were parted in still anticipation as his
touched them lightly, again and again, and then his

hand did start to move upward and the sudden explosion of her heart against her ribs was painful.

Ken's mouth covered hers and his hand tightened over her bare calf, fingers gently sliding and probing into the crease behind her knee, and Faith was trembling. The pressure that was aching in her abdomen and pushing against her chest was more than just arousal; it was need, a deep and overwhelming and desperate need for him, and it terrified her.

Her indrawn breath was a gasp when he lifted his mouth again slightly; it caught as a little sound of pain in Faith's throat. Ken made a soft sound against her cheek; she felt his lips there. His hand came up to stroke her hair, soothingly, and the other hand trailed slowly down her leg and away, leaving a trail of tingling absence in its wake.

Faith's heart was pounding a shattering counterpoint to the thin, jumpy flow of her breath, but even so she could feel the force of Ken's heart against her breast as he wrapped his arms around her and just held her for a minute, very close, hard-muscled and strong. Her knee, still curled beneath her on the sofa, felt the pressure of his thigh, her hands were unsteady against the heat of his back. It gradually came to her that the rush of his breathing, close to her ear, was uneven and tightly controlled. Everything within Faith was shaky, tenuous, about to crumble and fall. She concentrated all her strength into letting him go, into moving her hands away from his back, into stiffening her muscles, into trying to breathe normally.

Ken's hands cupped her face, fingers threading into

her hair, soothing her heated brow. Faith made herself open her eyes. Ken's face, faintly flushed and pleasure-softened, filled her vision. His smile was gentle and reassuring, but a little forced. The light of desire still heated his eyes, but beneath it was a subtle confusion, a hint of question. And Faith had to turn away from that question.

This was serious. This man—his presence in her life—was a very serious situation indeed. For so long she had held a clear picture of herself and what she wanted; now that self-image was blurring and her own goals and needs and the way they fit into her life were being turned upside down and twisted around, and it was the possibility of hope that was confusing her so. Her body responded to his touch the way it had to no other man's, the way she had never imagined it would. But worse, her mind and her heart were involved, twined around him somehow; he was seeping into the very core of her, and that she had never expected. She wanted him...perhaps to much. She did not know what to do.

Ken slowly let his hands drop from her face; he shielded his eyes with his lashes as he turned and sat beside her, facing straight ahead. If she could see his face, would there be disappointment or anger there? Something pulled painfully inside Faith's chest at the thought of seeing disappointment in Ken's eyes. She straightened her own legs and moved unobtrusively away from him, leaning into the corner of the sofa.

Ken was leaning forward slightly, with his arms resting on his thighs, hands clasped loosely between his knees. His profile was bland and relaxed, but Faith was hurting. What did he want from her? Sex? That would be easy enough to give... or it should have been. But Faith was terribly afraid that this time, with this man, it might cost her more than she could afford to lose. She didn't know what to do.

Ken looked thoughtfully at the cat, who returned his gaze without interest. "Well, Lance, old boy," he said out loud, "what you see before you is what is commonly known as a male dilemma, a curious phenomenon that develops more likely than not solely as a result of the human courtship ritual. And it looks as though I've come pretty close to blowing it.

"You see," he explained gently to a suddenly alert cat, "I want to be very careful not to hurt this lady, because she's extremely vulnerable right now. But to do that I have to somehow figure out what is best for her, and at the same time try to let her know that I still want her...."

Faith felt a small knot of something warm and tender begin to tighten in her stomach and she watched Ken cautiously, hardly breathing. "Being of the feline persuasion," Ken continued conversationally, "you probably don't understand this complicated mating process humans go through, but believe me, it's a very delicate business. You see, by nature, human beings are destined to choose a single mate and cleave to her, as it were, for a lifetime. Unfortunately, it is also within human nature to break all the rules, and in the process the mating ritual has become more of a recreation than a lifetime commitment, and there is a lot of suffering and disillusionment along the way. Naturally, given these circumstances, the adult male and female are going to be a little cautious in approaching each other. And here we come to my problem."

Ken paused, never once taking his eyes from the cat, and Lancelot yawned and stretched, then settled down patiently to hear the rest of the story. Faith's chest felt heavy with a warm and spreading emotion that wanted to reach out to him, to touch him or hold him—and was afraid to.

"How can I convince this woman that this is not just another part of the game, that I won't just use her for recreation and then discard her?" Ken inquired plainly of Lancelot. "You see, unlike the females of your own species, women need protecting and nourishing and a lot of care.... They weren't meant to be used and abandoned."

Faith's throat felt tight and sticky; her chest ached. Her hands closed slowly in her lap and she didn't dare breathe, or even blink. "But you've got to see her point of view," Ken continued mildly. "What does she know about me? Here's this jerk who just walks in off the street and starts making all kinds of heavy moves on her, and what is she supposed to think? But then on the other hand, here I am, trying to sell myself to this lady in every way I know how, and she's not exactly making it easy for me. She doesn't even date, for goodness' sake. So what am I supposed to do? I don't want to scare her off. I want to be straight with her. I know what I want, and sex is only a very, very small part of it. If I make love to her now, she won't understand, it will only confuse her more, and I don't want to cause her that kind of hurt. But there's no sense pretending I don't want to make love. So what do I do?''

Faith was aching from the inside out. She felt the hot sting of moisture on her lashes and she tried to blink it away, to swallow, to breathe normally. She was very much afraid she was beginning to fall in love with him.

Lancelot stood up, scratched his ear and settled back down again. Ken cocked his head intelligently. "What?" He made a wry face. "No, I can't tell her that. I told you, I don't want to scare her away. She'd never believe it anyway. Give the lady some credit for a little intelligence."

Lancelot yawned again, this time accompanying it with a muted yowl, and Ken gave him one last disparaging look. "You've got no class, cat. You'll have to come up with something better than that."

Ken turned to her, his smile gentle. "Your animal," he told her, "is not being much help."

Faith tried to smile. "What can you expect from a dumb cat?" she said thickly.

Ken's face softened with concern and tenderness; his thumb brushed lightly against her wet cheekbone. Faith flinched away because she knew if he touched her she would no longer be able to stop the tears. There was no reason for it, but if he touched her she would start to cry, and she might not be able to stop.

Worry lingered in Ken's eyes, though he smiled at her, trying to coax a response. "So, help me out, Faith," he said softly. "I'm trying not to rush things. It's too soon for you, I know. And I also know I can be very—" one corner of his lips tightened ruefully "—persuasive when I want to. I'm trying not to use that, and I'll back off whenever you tell me to. Do you want me to?"

Faith looked up at him, her eyes wide and searching, the faint glisten of tears that had sheened them slowly fading. She knew that he was telling the truth. There was such sincerity, such thoughtful concern in his eyes that she would have at that moment entrusted her very soul to his keeping, had he asked her. Did she want him to back off? She wasn't sure. For the first time in her life something reached out to her and glimmered with promise, and how could she turn away from that? But still there was so much . . .

"What do you want from me, Ken?" she asked. Her voice was hardly above a whisper, and her eyes never left his, trying to read the answer in his face before he said the words.

He thought about it a long time, hiding none of the process from her. He looked at her with tenderness and care, a patient reflection that seemed to enter her, lifting and examining the bits and pieces of her fragile heart and then gently replacing them, one by one, undisturbed. "I want," he told her soberly, "your happiness. And if that means—if for some crazy reason it really means—that I have to walk out of here tonight and never see you again, then that's what I'll do. I won't like it, but I'll do it."

Faith knew that he would. She also knew, with a quick faint leap of something that felt like alarm, that she did not want him to. And yet a small thread of despair tightened and pulled within her, signaling a warning bell she tried to ignore. It would never work. How could it work? *Oh, Ken,* she thought helplessly, *it's such a risk. You don't know what a risk.*

She made a small, uncertain motion with her hand, and he read the signal immediately. His own hand closed lightly about hers, and when she glanced at him, some of the anxiety was gone from his face. "Maybe," she said hesitantly, and afterward she would never be sure how she got the courage to say it, "maybe we could take some time...and get to know each other." But Ken would never know her, that persistent, nagging little voice accused her. There was an entire piece of her life, perhaps the most important piece, that Ken could never know. So what had she to offer him? What hope could there possibly be?

Later, Faith would regret not having listened to that voice. But that night she saw only the slow light of relief that rinsed Ken's eyes, felt only the warmth of his delighted smile, and was filled by the contentment in his voice as he said, "That's all I ever wanted, Faith. Truly." Then there was the unexpected mischief in his wink and he said, "I knew you'd see it my way." He settled back with a dramatic sigh of relief and released her hand. "I'll take that cocoa now," he said.

Faith laughed as she stood up to get the cups, and the burden that sailed from her then left her light enough to float, weightless, unfettered, carefree.

That night, Faith's only mistake was in listening to her heart.

Chapter Seven

Faith hung up the phone, a low and deadly fury kindling in her eyes. Her hands curled on the counter as though she wished they were around her worthy young assistant's throat. Late three days this week, out completely one, and now this...

Adrenaline quickened with an almost gleeful surge of anticipation as Faith saw the van draw up in front of the shop, and she came around the counter to greet Sally. The young girl was laughing and talking to someone, but Faith did not even notice that it was Ken Chapman who opened the door for the girl until Sally was inside and Faith was demanding, "Did you send an arrangement of carnations to Lois Greely this morning?"

Both Sally and Ken registered Faith's seething temper at once, and the laughter stopped. Ken threw his hands up in a quick defense of his innocence. "Not me," he denied.

The pleasure of seeing him almost overrode Faith's fury. She spared him no more than a quick glance, how-

ever, for she knew that anything more would completely neutralize her wrath and she would forget that
this time Sally had gone too far. No more second
chances. "Did you?" she demanded of the girl, un-
wavering.

Sally came cautiously into the shop, circling her employer like a wary animal who senses attack. "Well...
yes. I guess so."

Faith's eyes narrowed. "With a card that read 'Happy anniversary, darling, from your loving husband,
George'?"

Sally brightened a little, watching Faith as though
still expecting her to spring at any moment. "Sure,"
she said. "I remember that. I took the order."

"Mrs. Greely," Faith informed her tightly, "received a basket of forget-me-nots with a card that said
'Thank you for last night—all my love, Ralph.'"

Ken quickly brought his fist to his mouth to smother
a gulp of laughter, and Faith glared at him. He immediately sobered his expression, but his eyes twinkled
madly.

Sally's eyes widened in slow comprehension. "Ralph
Formby... he sent forget-me-nots to his girlfriend...
well, it was a busy day," she defended herself. "The
phone was ringing and all these orders coming in at
once and...I guess I got the orders mixed up," she
decided weakly. "Sorry."

"You guess you—!" Faith broke off, trying to remember to count to ten. She got to two. "George
Greely is ready to divorce his wife and beat up his
neighbor Ralph Martin—and all you can say is 'sorry'?

It's their wedding anniversary, for goodness' sake! Do you have any idea—"

"I said I was sorry," Sally interrupted sulkily. "What do you want from me, anyway?"

Faith took one slow, calming breath. "I want," she said simply, "your resignation."

Sally stared at her, eyes narrowing, a quick blotchy color creeping into her face. "Well, fine!" she said shrilly. "Fine with me. Who needs the hassle, anyway? I was going to quit anyway—on what you pay me, who needs it? You just mail me my check! I'm glad to get out!" She grabbed up her purse and swept past Ken, clanging the doorbell on her exit.

The shop rang with the unpleasantness of the encounter, and Faith squirmed under it. She hated scenes. She hated even more the fact that Ken had been there to witness it. She glanced at him uncomfortably, standing there with one elbow propped up on his folded arm, chin resting on his knuckles, looking deliberately sympathetic, but hiding, Faith suspected, a hard-fought mirth. She frowned at him. If he teased her now...

"I thought you handled that very well," Ken said soothingly.

Well, at least it was over. She had done it. Her severe expression faded into an awkward resignation, and she shrugged uncomfortably, turning to straighten a display that Sally's hasty exit had rearranged.

"Did you get the Greelys and the Formbys straightened out?" he asked soberly, but Faith was almost sure his eyes were dancing with repressed laughter.

"I think so," she muttered. "It wasn't easy, though."

He lost the valiant battle with his own sense of humor and the chuckle came bubbling through, then he was laughing, then he was doubled over, his shoulders shaking with it. Faith glared at him. "I'm sorry, darling," he gasped, "I really am, but—have you ever seen Lois Greely? She's a tiny silver-haired little thing in orthopedic shoes who wouldn't shoo a fly, and George—" Another spasm of laughter shook him and he clutched the counter to steady himself, his eyes shooting madly cavorting emerald sparks. "He's seventy-five years old and as thin as tissue paper, and Ralph Martin—" he practically hooted with laughter "—is a thirty-year-old ex-football player who weighs three hundred pounds, and the picture of those two going at it over mousy little Lois..." He collapsed helplessly against the wall.

Faith's lips twitched hard as she tried to maintain her severe stance. She turned away quickly and busied herself with a stack of order forms, but hidden from Ken by her severely squared shoulders, a wide grin had broken out and laughter was bubbling in her eyes.

Five silver-pink roses had joined the ones in the vase on Faith's kitchen table since the evening she and Ken had walked in the rain. Ken had become a familiar presence around the flower shop. He wandered in once or twice a day and stayed for a few minutes or a few hours. Occasionally he brought her lunch from the drugstore or from the health-food store on the other side of town, which featured such marvelously healthy things as alfalfa sprouts on carrot bread and yogurt shakes. Once, as she opened up the shop, he surprised her with orange juice and Danish. And every time Faith looked up and saw his familiar smile falling over her, it was a jolt to her pulses, a quick soaring of delighted surprise, an infusion of sunlight. Perhaps part of Ken's charm lay in his unpredictability.

Usually when he visited, Faith was very busy, and that disturbed her because they had very little time actually to spend together. On one of the busiest afternoons Faith could remember he stayed three entire hours, and Faith barely had time to say hello to him between customers. He stayed placidly in the background, out of her way, sometimes exchanging a few words with the customers, watching her work. Finally Faith said to him in a mixture of puzzlement and apology, "I don't understand—why do you want to hang around here all day when we don't even get a chance to talk to each other?"

Ken smiled and replied simply, "I just want to give you a chance to get used to having me around."

It was a harum-scarum courtship, if, indeed, that was what it was. A few minutes here and there, afternoons spent in a place of public business with random interruptions of whatever conversation they might have started, a rose for hope every day...and not a single minute spent alone together. As usual, Faith was confused. She knew no more about him now than she had on the rainy evening she had eavesdropped on his conversation with the cat, and he certainly knew nothing about her. But one thing she did know, and very clearly: she liked having Ken in her life.

"What are you doing here, anyway?" Faith tossed over her shoulder now, when both had had a chance to recover themselves somewhat. She stacked a pile of delivery sheets and slipped them under the counter. "Don't you ever work?"

Ken looked at her thoughtfully. "As a matter of fact, I do. Would you like to see my work? Yes." And with a quick, decisive motion that was very typical of him, he grabbed up her purse, flipped the Closed sign on the door, and crossed the room to catch her wrist. "That's exactly what you'd like to do."

Faith stared at him, protesting as he pulled her around the counter, "Ken, are you crazy? I can't leave! I just fired my only assistant, I—"

"Perfect, you deserve to celebrate." He was bundling her out the door. "You're going to love this; it might even solve all your problems—and a few of mine, too." He locked the door behind them.

It wasn't until Faith was securely seat-belted into Ken's car that she realized why she had not put up a greater fight. It struck her first as amusing, then as vaguely disturbing, that she had known this man for over a week, and that he had come to play a very important part in her life—invading her dreams and her private thoughts, lingering on the outskirts of everything she did in her waking hours, working subtle changes in the way she saw herself and her life—but that Faith did not have the slightest idea what he did for a living. It wasn't that she hadn't wondered about it—about how he did appear to be able to make his own hours, for example—but she had never asked and he had never volunteered. Perhaps she hadn't asked because she felt the more she knew of him the more real he would become, and the less easily she would be able to keep him as a vague and unthreatening fantasy figure. Perhaps she didn't ask because at this point it would be awkward; she never asked Ken anything personal about himself because she didn't want to admit, even secretly, how badly she wanted to know everything about him.

He drove out of town on the state highway for about five miles, and the close community of neatly kept turn-of-the-century homes gave way to farmhouses and meadows, swaying fields of new fescue, barbed-wire road frontage and cows and freshly tilled soil. It smelled wonderful, and Faith filled her eyes with the scenery and the scents, letting the tension of the awful scene with Sally wash away with the breeze from her open window.

Ken gave her a running commentary on the history of the area, and then Faith asked her first personal question. "How long have you lived here?"

"As an adult? I was sent here three years ago, but my dad worked in South Bend before he retired, and we lived there most of the time I was in high school. That's how Amelia—my sister—met her husband."

Faith was about to comment on the coincidence of his returning as an adult to a town so near the place where he had spent his adolescent years, but Ken signaled a turn just then off the highway and onto a well-maintained dirt drive. A sign hanging from an iron post at the entrance announced: The Crossroads.

Faith turned to read it, and Ken made a wry face. "The name wasn't my idea—it's kind of corny, but appropriate, I suppose."

Faith turned back to him, filled with curiosity now, to ask what, exactly, the sign was appropriate for, and he stopped the car in front of a large, sprawling, two-story Victorian house. "Here we are," he announced.

The house must have at one time been a mansion of some repute. Its double turrets, wide bay windows and gingerbread latticework testified to a builder of wealth and taste. Now every inch of the house—even the bricks—was painted a bright, eye-stinging buttercup yellow. And over that color were works of art of unquestionable skill, if uncertain taste—huge sunflowers flanking the front door, a gargantuan unicorn galloping around the side porch, a rainbow gracing the second story and pouring its beneficent light over all. There were other panels—Faith caught a glimpse of a crowd scene on the other side of the house, a seascape of some sort beneath an upper-story window, and it all was such a breathtaking riot of color and design that for a moment she was speechless.

Ken was grinning at her. "Well, what do you think?"

Faith ventured a little weakly, "You paint houses?"

Ken laughed and got out of the car. "We had a budding young artist here a couple of years ago—right after the place opened," he explained as he opened her door. "Everything you see here is compliments of restless energy and repressed talent. I got a letter from him

last winter," Ken added, with a note of unmistakable
pride. "He has a job with Disney Studios now."

Faith got out of the car and walked with Ken up the
wide veranda, her senses working in busy counterpoint
with her mind to try to absorb it all. "Most of the kids
are still in school," he explained, "or at work. Those
are two things we insist upon—that everyone have
some kind of part-time job, and that they stay in
school."

The front door was splashed with a replica of the
rainbow over the porch, and Ken opened it onto a
wide, airy foyer carpeted in brick linoleum. A double-
banistered maple staircase ascended from the far corner, mismatched chairs, hassocks and occasional tables
were scattered around along with a number of lamps
and magazine stands. From a room that opened off the
foyer the sounds of a television floated, and the walls
breathed the aroma of something good cooking in the
kitchen.

"Of course," Ken continued, leading the way across
the room, "all the kids have assigned chores around
here, too. We have our own garden out back and, with
a place this size, there's always plenty of yard work to
be done—not to mention kitchen and cleaning duties.
You'd be amazed," he said with a slow shake of his
head, "how shocked some of the kids are when they
first discover they have to work for their keep. But after
a while they stop resenting it and actually fight over the
jobs—it gives them pride, and a sense of belonging, to
know they're responsible for something. I sometimes
think a lot of them wouldn't be here in the first place if

someone had only taken the time to teach them things like self-pride and responsibility."

They came into a wide room that was furnished as a recreation room: long couches and well-worn easy chairs were scattered around; there was a pool table in the center, a stereo set, a chess table set up in one corner, and a television tuned to an afternoon soap opera. Before it, with jeaned legs swung over the arm of a sagging, slipcovered chair, reposed a girl whom Faith took at one glance to be somewhere between fifteen and thirty-five. She wore her dark brown hair loose, with one section pulled up on the side in a sexy ponytail; her eyes were smeared with dark teal shadow and caked with mascara; her lips were a glossy cherry-red. Her jeans were tight enough to pop at the seams, and her red-and-white-striped T-shirt, fashionably oversized and off the shoulder, bared an appreciable portion of her left breast. She wore red plastic hoop earrings that touched her shoulders and dangled one stiletto-heeled shoe from her big toe as she rested her legs across the chair.

"Well, well," Ken said as they entered the room. "Here we have one member of the tribe who is neither at work nor at school. What's the problem, Chelsy?"

The girl glanced up indolently at his entrance and reached deliberately for a cigarette from the pack at her side. Her long, pointed nails were painted purple. "Cramps," she replied, and lit the cigarette. But Faith noticed a certain wariness within her rudely negligent manner. Chelsy never took her eyes off Ken.

Ken lifted an eyebrow. "Hmm. I guess I'd better go

dig out my old biology textbooks. Seems to me you've been out with cramps three times this month."

Chelsy did not flinch. "So I got a weird biology."

Ken smiled and turned to Faith. "Chelsy, I want you to meet a friend of mine, Faith Hilliard. Faith, this is Chelsy Warren."

The girl looked her over once, and then broke into a wide, not entirely unfriendly grin. "Hey, is she your woman? I didn't think guys like you were allowed."

"Watch your mouth, Chelsy," Ken warned pleasantly, and gave her ponytail a gentle tweak that made her squeal, more from insult than injury, and more from pleasure than resentment. "And get your biology straightened out," he advised. "You've got too much at stake to blow it now."

The girl took a drag on the cigarette, shrugged away from him, and turned her eyes back to the television set. "It's boring," she complained around a cloud of gray smoke. "Stupid and boring. All we ever do is study hall, anyway. What do I have to go for? I'm not learning nothing."

"You could learn," Ken suggested, "that double negatives are not considered a proper form of speech." She shot him a damning glare, but Ken looked at her thoughtfully. "What would you think about cutting out those study halls, having morning classes, and working in the afternoons?"

Chelsy frowned at him suspiciously. "Ain't got no job," she replied, and deliberately blew a puff of smoke his way. Obviously, she was coarsening her speech to get back at him for the comment about double negatives.

Ken agreed, "That is a problem." He checked his watch before turning back to Faith, then glanced at the television. "Your show is over in fifteen minutes," he said. "I expect you in the kitchen to help Mrs. Allen. And that," he said with a sweet smile but a tone that left no doubt he was serious, "is an order."

Chelsy leaned forward and deliberately turned up the volume on the television set.

Ken touched Faith's arm lightly to lead her from the room. "We get all kinds of kids here," he explained under cover of the television set. "Drug problems, behavior problems, thievery, assault, the discards and debris of teenage society."

"It's a halfway house," Faith realized, slowly understanding. And it made perfect, beautiful sense. Ken, a social worker. She should have guessed it all along.

Ken smiled at her. "Not exactly. We try to get them before they get halfway. It's hard to get the jail out of the kid once he's been there," Ken said, and a peculiar, troubled, almost hurt expression crossed his eyes. "We try to keep them from ever getting there—to give them another choice."

Faith asked the one question that had been bothering her since entering the room. "You don't say anything about her smoking?" she asked, and then realized immediately it was none of her business.

One corner of Ken's mouth turned upward in an amused half-grin. "Why should I? She'll put it out as soon as we leave the room. She doesn't even inhale, didn't you notice?"

Faith glanced over her shoulder, and sure enough,

Chelsy was already stubbing out the barely touched cigarette, waving at a cloud of smoke. Faith smiled. "You know your business," she agreed.

Ken led the way across the linoleum foyer again. "Now Chelsy," he explained, "is what they call an incorrigible. A persistent runaway. She has no real problems except an uneasy relationship with authority and a pretty low self-esteem. I think a lot of that could be solved if she had a job."

Ken glanced at her, and understanding slowly began to dawn. But he forestalled any comment Faith might have liked to make by opening another door and introducing her to the reading room.

Ken took her on a tour of the entire building, the girls' and boys' dormitories upstairs, the two private study chambers, the communal dining room, ending at last in the enormous kitchen, where a plump, salt-and-pepper-haired woman in jeans and a gray sweatshirt sat at the worktable, mixing a huge bowl of cookie batter.

"And this," Ken introduced, grinning, "is the heart and soul of the entire operation. Mickie Allen, meet Faith Hilliard. How's it going, Mick?" The woman looked up with a friendly smile, and Ken brushed her cheek with a kiss. She slapped at his hand as a finger dipped quickly into the cookie batter, but Ken escaped with a grin, licking the dough off his fingers and making appreciative sounds. The woman frowned and scolded him, then offered him a spoon.

"This one's the biggest kid of all," she complained to Faith as Ken dipped his spoon into the bowl. "I have to put guards at the door when I'm baking my chocolate pies."

"How many children do you have here?" Faith asked, with interest.

"Twelve right now," Mickie answered, "but we have had up to twenty." She chuckled. "Things get a little tight around here, then, let me tell you." And she smiled at Faith warmly. "We can use all the help we can get."

Faith gave Ken a suspicious look of quiet reprimand, which he cheerfully ignored. He explained, licking the spoon with defiant delight, "Mickie and her husband, Bill, are our live-in houseparents. Of course, we have daily volunteers who come in on a part-time basis, and professional counselors who contribute their time, but these two are the only thing that really keeps the place together."

"Aw, go on with you," Mickie mumbled, disguising her pleasure with tightening lips and an increased vigor applied to the stirring spoon. "And get out of my kitchen while I've still got some batter left for cookies."

Ken grinned and dipped his spoon into the bowl one more time, then their attention was caught by a disturbance outside the window. Mickie turned toward the sound of angry voices, and Ken lifted an eyebrow. "Tony and Bob again?"

Mickie sighed, getting up and going toward the door. Her pretty plump face was creased with worry. "I don't know what I'm going to do with those two. They're disrupting the whole house, and pretty soon it's going to get to where I can't handle it—"

A burst of violent obscenity floated into the room, and Faith looked at Ken in alarm. Those two sounded as if they meant business. Ken licked the rest of the batter off the spoon and placed the spoon on the table, going casually to the back door. Mrs. Allen followed him, and in a minute so did Faith.

Two young boys faced each other in an angry stand-off in the backyard. One was blond and sporting the proud beginnings of a scrubby beard; the other was short and wiry, with sullen dark eyes that looked at that moment as though they would like to kill. He held a hoe in his hands, and everything about his stance indicated nothing would dissuade him from using it as a weapon. Near them was a sizable piece of tilled ground that was beginning to show green with the tops of carrots and beans and the viny leaves of potatoes and tomatoes; behind them opened a sweep of picturesque lawn and oak trees. Punching bags, tire swings, and other forms of recreational equipment marred the pastoral beauty of the landscape, along with a badminton net and a trampoline.

Ken went down the three concrete steps from the back stoop and crossed in unhesitant strides toward the two boys. Just as he reached them the dark-eyed boy whirled on him with a vicious swing of the hoe, shouting, "Keep the hell out of this!"

Faith's heart, as well as her hand, flew to her throat as Ken caught the handle of the hoe in one hand just before its blade struck his face. The force was enough to jar the muscles of his arm. It all happened so quickly, so unexpectedly, that it took a moment for the shock

waves to hit Faith. When they did she found herself
thinking a little wildly, *Those kids aren't fooling! He
would have hit him, that crazy boy would have really hit
Ken with that hoe and might have killed him.* She felt the
pressure of her heart settling into a painful contraction
and expanding in the center of her chest, and her fingers
were numb. She couldn't believe what had almost happened. She couldn't believe what she had seen.

One thing was very clear, though: the hatred in the
dark eyes that faced Ken across the hoe handle. He'd
do it again, thought Faith incredulously. He may yet.
Ken's back was to her, and she could not see the expression on his face. She did see the muscles of his
arm, bare beneath the sleeve of his T-shirt, clench and
harden, she saw a small film of perspiration begin to
sheen the young boy's face and the taut muscles of his
own arms begin to quiver, and that was the only sign of
the silent struggle of incredible strength that went on
over possession of the weapon.

Then, at last, with a hissing oath, the boy released
his hold; Ken tossed the hoe silently aside. Still Faith
could not see Ken's face and she was burning to. His
voice was very mild, but Faith had the most disturbing
suspicion that whatever was in his eyes was something
she had never seen before, and she was not entirely
certain she wanted to. It was something that made the
two boys, livid with anger only moments ago, eventually drop their eyes and loose their rigidity and begin to
shuffle uncomfortably in place.

"Okay," Ken said easily, "I'm ready. I'll take you
on; one at a time." He looked first to the blond boy.
"Bob? Let's have at it."

The one called Bob spat on the ground, shoved his hands in his pockets, and shrugged, staring at a far tree. "Nah, man..." he mumbled at last. "Ain't interested."

Ken turned to the dark-eyed boy. "What's the matter, Tony?" he challenged quietly. Though his stance was relaxed, his voice unconcerned, Faith noticed that he had never completely turned his back on the boy and his hands were curled slightly at his sides, ready to defend himself. Ken was no fool. Faith's admiration for him and awe of him swelled and soared unexpectedly, filling all of her. She was right, she knew hardly anything about Ken, but everything she learned was more and more fascinating.

"Afraid you can't take me?" Ken prodded the boy. "Come on, give it a shot. Or don't you think you'd have a chance without a piece of wood and metal to protect you?"

For a moment Faith thought Ken had gone too far. The hatred in the boy's eyes flared; he clenched his fists convulsively. The moment of eye contact lasted forever, and then Tony relaxed his fists and shifted his gaze away. "Man, I wouldn't waste my sweat on scum like you," he spat, and whirled away.

Ken caught him abruptly by the shoulder, turning him around and immediately releasing him. "All right," he said, and jerked his head curtly to Bob. "Hit the punching bags, both of you. You act like children, you're going to be treated like children. But before you do, think about this."

Both boys stopped suspiciously before him. Ken's voice was a little harsh. "You guys have got enough problems without this kind of garbage. You've got the cops breathing down your necks and no place to go from here. You've got a teenage unemployment rate of forty-eight percent, and neither one of you idiots could keep a job if you could find it. You've got friends who are buying concert tickets at thirty dollars a shot and driving racy little Corvettes and going off to college and don't you think you'd like a piece of that action every once in a while? Is this what you really want for your lives, because believe me, it's all downhill from here. Why don't you spend a little less energy trying to kill each other and a little more trying to get your acts together and then you come see me. Because I'll tell you the truth, it's getting to the point where neither of you kids is worth the time it takes me to tell you to shove it. Now go on." He jerked his head shortly in the direction of the punching bags. "Get."

It was only another moment before the two boys turned sharply and left him, and the sound of bare fists against punching bags was ringing in the air before Faith saw the hard square of Ken's shoulders relax. He turned and came back to her.

His smile was dryly amused and almost natural, but there was a lingering edge of tension in his eyes as he came up the steps. "You handled that very well," Faith said, echoing his earlier words to her.

Ken's lift of an eyebrow was half-apologetic. "Sometimes," he explained, "diplomacy is not enough. Sometimes, as a matter of fact, I think I'd make a lot more progress with a two-by-four than with an inspirational speech."

Faith smiled as Ken took her arm and led her back through the kitchen. Mickie, who had returned to her cookies as soon as the crisis was over, called out with a friendly wave, "Come see us again, Miss Hilliard," and Faith returned her smile warmly. She had the definite suspicion that that was more than within the realm of likelihood.

"You do good work here, Ken," Faith said quietly as they reached the foyer, and she meant it. It amazed her all over again that there was this whole new dimension to Ken she had never even guessed at before. He was unfolding before her, slowly but surely, and each new discovery was almost overwhelmingly wonderful. How had this man come into her life? How could she, Faith Hilliard, with nothing but a record of losses and bad judgments behind her, have been so fortunate? It made her feel humble, wondering, a little in awe.

Ken's smile was vague, slightly self-deprecating. "It's a fifty-fifty proposition. For some of the kids this is just a stopping place on the way to a life of crime and nothing we can say or do can help them. Sometimes I feel like a doctor who knows there's nothing he can do to save his patient but gives it his best shot anyway— and loses. It's frustrating. More than that."

His tone had grown quiet, a shadow crossed his face. Faith watched him alertly, everything within her straining toward him, wanting to share with him, becoming a part of him and the deep commitment he felt to his work. "When a doctor loses a patient," he explained, still very thoughtfully, "it's over; no second chances, no point in wondering what you did wrong or wishing

you had acted differently. But when I lose one..."
Faith had the feeling he was trying to explain it to himself as much as to her. The lines around his mouth
were tight, reflecting remembered pain. "When I let
one slip away, it's only the beginning. When these kids
leave here unchanged, they walk straight into a living
hell filled with torn-up lives and twisted minds, crime,
poverty, alcoholism, drug addiction—they'll die a violent death at a young age and take who knows how
many innocent victims with them, or they'll rot in prison with all the hope gone out of their eyes."

Ken's arm had been entwined lightly with hers; now
she felt his distress penetrate her with a slight increase
of the pressure of his fingers on her wrist. His eyes
were bleak as he stared into that picture of horror, and
his voice weary. "What a responsibility, Faith," he said
in a low voice. "What an awful responsibility."

He made her understand. He made her feel it as he
did, and Faith cared, because he did. She wanted to
tell him so, she wanted to let him know that her heart
was filled with him and with the suffering he felt for
children that were not even his own. She wanted suddenly to touch his shiny brown hair in a gesture of
tenderness and reassurance, to smooth the troubled
lines from his brow. She wanted him to know that she
cared.

Then Ken glanced at her, and smiled quickly, again
almost apologetically. "But sometimes," he told her,
and the smile that touched his lips gradually began to
find its way to his eyes, "sometimes we do something
right. Sometimes being here makes a difference, and

some kid leaves here with something he didn't have when he started, and then I think, we won one this time." The corners of his mouth deepened with the reflection of fierce triumph, his voice low and intense and satisfied. "Thank God, we won one. And that," he told her, his face lightening into a full smile as he looked at her, "is the best feeling in the world."

You are wonderful, Ken Chapman, Faith thought, and surely that sentiment, which seemed to begin in her toes and glow throughout her whole body, was reflected in Faith's eyes. *You are simply wonderful.*

The need to touch him, to hold him, to be close to him in the physical as well as the emotional sense was becoming almost overpowering, filling her and radiating from her. Ken must have seen it, because his face softened as he looked at her, a new and subtle light flickered in his eyes, and his hand on her arm tightened slightly, and he made a small motion as though to turn her to him, before apparently remembering where they were and the curious eyes that might be watching. Both regret and a promise were in his eyes as he gestured her forward, remarking, "I suppose you're wondering why I brought you here."

Faith's lips tightened with sly amusement. Ken Chapman, wonderful as he was, still had a great deal to learn about subtlety. "Why, to impress me with your noble nature and humanitarian deeds, of course," she replied.

His eyes sparkled down at her as they stepped out into the sunlight. "And...?" he prompted.

"And it never hurts to have the business community

aware of a project like this." Their steps crunched on the hard-packed earth of the driveway.

"More specifically?"

She stopped before the car, looking up at him. Her eyes were twinkling gently. "You want me to hire one of your kids for my shop."

"Give the lady a cigar," he declared, his own eyes dancing. He hooked his fingers into the front pockets of his jeans, rocking back on his heels, watching her with easy mirth. The sun sparked in his hair and squinted his eyes. "Well?"

Just like that. This man didn't believe in the soft sell, that much was for certain. Did he have any idea what could be involved in such a move? Faith had no experience working with underprivileged children; she wasn't a psychologist. She had just gotten over a horrible experience with an unsatisfactory employee, and she had her business to consider. Faith wanted to help, she would have loved to say yes, but did Ken have any idea what he was asking?

She let her eyes wander over his shoulder to the whimsically painted, gaily colored building behind them. So like Ken. Rainbows and unicorns, mysteries and miracles... Impossible deeds accomplished with the twinkle of an eye and a few compact sentences. How incredible this man was, how in awe she was of him. How much she wanted to be a part of his rainbow-colored world. And how easy it would be to let herself be drawn into it.

As she hesitated, Ken leapt in, as he always did, to seize the moment. "Look at it this way," he persuaded easily. "You're getting fresh material, to train as you please. A business like yours is perfect for this project because it provides room for a creative outlet as well as work discipline. And best yet, you don't even have to pay minimum wage. In fact, unless the job involves hard physical labor or developed skills, we prefer that you don't. A girl like Chelsy, for example..."

Faith glanced up at him suspiciously. "Chelsy?" Not only had he volunteered her services as an employer, he had already picked out her employee. What did one do with a man like Ken Chapman? A little voice whispered back, *Just adore him*....

Ken nodded enthusiastically. "Perfect for you. She knows the town, has a driver's license, and believe it or not, is a very organized young lady behind that mask of twelve-day-old makeup. She's bright, too, which is exactly why she's bored with school. This could be the perfect solution for her. And as I was saying, I think a dollar fifty to two dollars an hour would be adequate compensation; noon to closing six days a week, and full-time when school lets out next month."

"Ken, I don't know," Faith ventured once, a little desperately. "There could be so many problems."

But Ken had already made up her mind for her. "All you have to do is give it a try," he insisted placidly. "We don't want any special treatment. The first screwup, the first sign of a bad attitude or a disciplinary problem, you fire her, just like you would any other employee. And if you don't have the heart to do it," Ken volunteered generously, "I will. It's as important for these kids to learn the consequences of their own failures as it is for them to have a chance to reap the rewards of success. You don't really have anything to lose."

Faith looked at Ken for a long moment, thoughtfully. What a fascinating man he was. How full of hidden depths and surprising motivations, and everything about him intrigued Faith...as it had from the first, but more now than ever. "Why do you do it, Ken?" she asked at last, curiously. "Why this?" She gestured to the building behind them. "Why Chelsy, and Tony, and all the others? How did you choose this kind of work?"

His smile was brief and tight, and it did not quite reach his eyes. "Maybe it chose me," he said. And then he shrugged. "Growing up is hard enough as it is. It shouldn't have to be done from the inside of a jail."

And his eyes grew slowly opaque; his range of vision seemed to include something just beyond the top of her head. "Bad things happen to kids in jail," he said. "Kids get raped in jail, beaten. They learn how to carve spoons into weapons just so they can sleep at night, and they learn how to smuggle drugs in body cavities and then trade them for protection. They learn how to steal and kill and terrorize from the best in the business. They learn how to fight for their lives, literally. And when they go back on the streets they don't have a chance because the poison has worked its way into their minds."

His voice had been slowly gaining passion, a low ferocity that almost frightened Faith. Now he deliberately caught himself. He took a breath and looked back at her, and the cloudy screen that had obscured his eyes was gone. "So, I try to work a deal with the judge and the prosecutor and the parents to give us a shot at them first. That's the only way we have a chance—if we can get to them while they still have something to lose, before they've seen the worst. And we try to keep the punitive undertones that are associated with 'reform school' and 'work farm' out of it. We're pretty loose around here; just a few rules but absolutely no exceptions. The kids know that when they come, and they know the consequences if they break the rules aren't always up to me. So they have a choice, and while they're here, the responsibility and the freedom to make it. Sometimes," he explained, "the judge will let them work off a fine for the city while living here. Sometimes the parents send their kids to me voluntarily, like Chelsy's folks. And sometimes this is the only alternative to a hard-core jail sentence." He shrugged. "As I said, we get all kinds of kids for all kinds of reasons." And then he smiled suddenly, dazzlingly, and demanded, "So. What about Chelsy? Does she have a job?"

Faith looked at him helplessly, and gradually a small smile of resignation began to tighten her lips. "So if Chelsy and I have a big blowup and I fire her, will you get mad at me and never see me again?"

Ken paused with his hand on the door handle, a lovely softness muting his eyes, a sweet, speculative smile shadowing his lips. "Would you mind that?" he inquired with gentle intensity. "Would it bother you if I never saw you again?"

More than you know, Faith thought suddenly, and the

realization startled her. More, perhaps, than even she yet knew. She lowered her eyes quickly, turning to get into the car, and returned brightly, "Sure it would. I hate to have a dissatisfied customer, and you'd be out ninety-three dollars and ninety-six cents on roses."

Ken looked at her for a long time, his hand resting on the door handle. His eyes were on fire with sunlight and tenderness and a deep, steady flicker of contentment and desire, and Faith felt herself begin to melt beneath that gaze. Then, as though afraid the moment was growing too intense, he smiled at her quickly and closed her door.

What signals, Faith wondered, was she sending out that always made him back away? Especially since, she realized without warning, that was really the last thing she wanted him to do. Since that one night at her house, Ken had been very careful never to see her alone or in any place that could remotely present a chance for intimacy. Was he protecting her, or himself, from feelings that were escalating too fast? And why was there this strange sense of disappointment within Faith now as she saw yet another moment slip away?

The answer stole slowly over Faith, decision that had been made so easily and naturally that she had hardly noticed when it had happened. Over the days, culminating perhaps in the events of this past hour, something had been changing within Faith, slowly evolving, a gentle surprise that she welcomed, rather than fought. She wanted Ken. She did not know what would happen, she did not know what their chances were or how she would handle the obstacles that lay ahead. Faith had a right to choose her own life, and she chose a life with Ken Chapman in it.

Ken inserted his key into the ignition, shooting her a quick, bemused glance. "You have a strange look on your face," he observed. "What are you thinking?"

Faith smiled, not troubling to hide the look he had already seen. The sweep of happiness that radiated within her felt like a beacon, and surely he could guess the reason for it. "Oh," she said, leaning back comfortably in the seat, "I was just thinking how incredible you are."

His low chuckle hid whatever surprise might have registered with that unexpected comment as he started the ignition. "Love it, love it. Tell me more."

Faith's eyes were sparkling with hidden mirth and a secret wellspring of excitement that seemed to be generated by nothing more than his presence. She folded her hands casually in her lap and glanced at him askance. "Well," she began, sounding suitably impressed, "here you are, a single, unattached male in the prime of his life, a perfect physical specimen...." She caught a glint in his eye, which she pretended to ignore as he put the car in gear. She continued implacably, "You don't drink, smoke or swear, you send me roses; you're a certified cooler expert and animal hypnotist...." He gave a small, modest bow of his head as they pulled out onto the highway, and Faith's eyes sparked. Beneath his playful bravado Faith thought she was really beginning to embarrass him, and she loved it. "You're gentle, considerate, thoughtful..."

"The kind of guy you'd love to take home to

Mother," he supplied helpfully, and Faith enthusiastically agreed.

"And to top all that, you devote your life to helping
underprivileged youth, and you're really good at it."
Now she was serious. "You really care, Ken. There
aren't many people left in the world who care about
anything, but you give it all you've got. It amazes
me."

Now it was no longer speculation that he was embarrassed, and Faith registered the fact with a new surge of
delight. His laugh was a little uncomfortable, and there
was the very faintest hint of a flush warming his
cheeks. "You make me sound like a saint," he objected, and was paying a lot of attention to the road on
which the automobile traveled at a sedate thirty-five
miles per hour.

"In a way," Faith admitted slowly, "I guess you are.
I mean, let's face it, you've got more virtues than most
people have vices, and that's a little intimidating. Almost too good to be true."

One corner of his mouth dropped with a tight,
crooked smile, and he seemed tense. He did not take
his eyes off the road. "I wouldn't go that far. I have my
share of faults."

"Like what?" inquired Faith curiously, turning to
look at him more closely. In the time they had spent
together, up to and including today, Faith had learned
more about him than she had ever learned about anyone, and among the long list of attributes and charac-
teristics she could ascribe to Ken Chapman not one
could be categorized as a fault. What did he consider

his own weaknesses and failings? That was the one thing that had always been missing from her assessment of Ken, and Faith had the feeling that the only way she would ever find out was if he told her.

"I have a ferocious temper," he admitted after a time, "which I hope you never have to see." His voice was quiet, and serious, and Faith found that confession hard to believe. The last thing she would have ever credited this placid man with was a temper. "I almost lost it with those boys this afternoon," he said, "and when that happens I get furious with myself, which only makes it worse." He laughed a little, but it was not a happy sound. "I can be one mean guy when I get mad," he said, "so I have to work very hard to keep from getting mad. That's pretty imperfect of me, wouldn't you say?"

He shrugged, not giving her a chance to answer. "And you make my work sound so noble, but it's not, really. There's a lot of pride involved, a lot of personal ego. I take too much of the credit for success on myself and forget to give it where it really belongs ... that's not good. I'm very possessive," he informed her with a glance, "impulsive, stubborn, overbearing and ..." His stern recitation relaxed into a half-grin. "Believe it or not, even a little domineering at times. I like to have my own way and I know how to use my charming personality to get it, which isn't very nice of me. I'm pretty self-centered when it comes right down to it; I like to be in control. Am I starting to sound like something less than the paragon you thought I was?"

Faith looked at him thoughtfully, smiling. "It really

makes you uncomfortable, doesn't it, to be thought of as a good man?''

Ken's profile was sober, his eyes unreadable. "Only because I'm not."

Faith shook her head slowly, that clear, wondering smile never leaving her eyes. "You'll have to do better than that to convince me."

Suddenly the car bounced over the uneven shoulder of the road, tires spraying gravel; the car jerked to a halt. Ken caught Faith under the arms and hauled her breathless form across the seat to him, eyes gleaming with wicked mischief, and declared throatily, "How about a little ravishment? Would that convince you?"

He began to rain violent kisses over her face and neck and shoulders, and Faith squealed with laughter, struggling playfully and striking at him until his own laughing lips accidently brushed across hers and then captured them in a full and deep and totally unexpected kiss. The laughter died in her throat with the sudden catch of her breath, and her hands, which had been pummeling his shoulders, clasped them now instead for support against a swift and sweeping weakness.

The next sound that escaped her was a tiny moan as he started to lift his head; her hands were against his neck, pressing him back to her. Faith felt his catch of breath as she kissed him, tentatively at first, then more assertively, her tongue flickering across his mouth, gently drawing his lower lip between her teeth, caressing him as he did her, giving to him as he was giving constantly to her. His thumbs moved in a circular motion with ever-increasing pressure against her breasts, regulating the pounding rhythm of her pulse, the tightening of his fingers on her back drawing her ever closer as his mouth covered hers, his tongue invaded her and the hot sweep of sudden passion blinded her.

His hands moved to her face, fingers driving into her hair and tightening on her skull. He turned her head to allow him fuller access to her mouth, and it was as though he wanted to devour her, to possess her fully and for all time with the strength of this one kiss. Faith was lost in him, helpless to do anything but pull him closer, meeting the power of his desire with her own. She felt the searing heat of a thousand corpuscles opening her skin to him; she felt moist sensuous motions of his tongue inside her mouth and the slow, mind-stripping drawing and sucking motions of his lips upon hers; she felt the tingling pulse of aching desire low in her body; she felt her thighs loosening for him. She could feel the pressure of Ken's body against hers, and she could imagine herself arching to meet him, wrapping her legs about him, drawing him to her, holding him tightly, and the power of it was so strong it shook her. It was as though this were the first time she had ever felt like this... perhaps it was the first time.

"Faith..." The syllable was hardly a whisper as he touched dewy, sun-lightened kisses over her heated cheek, her swollen lips, her chin, her nose. His hands stroked her hair, urgently, repetitively, from forehead to neck and back again, memorizing the shape of her head. "Lovely Faith..." She could hear the jerk of his own heartbeat in his voice.

Faith drew in her breath sharply as his lips found her

neck, her fingers tightened on his shoulders. "I'm also," he breathed, "unpredictable..." He nibbled at her collarbone. "Impatient..." His tongue flicked and darted around her ear, and his voice came to Faith in a swirling haze. "And..." Faith gasped out loud, but it sounded more like a moan of surrender as his lips traveled around her neck, down her throat, pressing at last into the V-shaped square of flesh between her breasts exposed by her open collar. "Badly lacking in self-control."

And then, very slowly, he gathered her to him, burying his face in her neck, holding her tightly but with exquisite care. Faith could feel the slight quiver in the muscles of his arms, and she was reminded dartingly, irrationally, of the strength in a single one of those arms that had held off the killing rage of a violent young boy this afternoon. "Oh, Faith," he whispered. The words were a hot moist rush against her oversensitized flesh. "Don't let me lose control now...."

The words to Faith were at first hazy, disjointed, reaching her from a distance and barely penetrating the barrier of misty red passion that enfolded her. Control was beyond her reach. He had taken it with his first embrace, weakened it with his first smile, captured it in the power of his eyes. The need for him was her only awareness, just to be with him and belong to him for however short a time...and then it came to her, what he had said, what it meant. She wanted to make love to him in a car parked by the side of the road in broad daylight, to give her body unthinkingly to him for nothing more than the pleasure of it; she had lost control.

She was feeling it, wanting him, and the realization was devastating, mind-boggling, unacceptable.

Her senses returned to her in a slow, downward spiraling motion as Ken's arms slowly released her, as he made himself push away from her. How had this happened, when had it come to this, what did it mean? How had her life, in one sweeping motion, gotten so completely turned around? What was this man doing to her?

Faith looked into his eyes for an answer, but Ken's smile was a little weak, the hand that stroked her hair one last time somewhat unsteady. He sat back slowly against the seat, facing straight ahead. The slow, deliberate pace of his breathing was audible, and for a long time that was the only sound.

He had left her shaken, disjointed, and aching with a low vague physical pain that was like sandpaper rubbing across raw nerve endings. Faith had never felt like this before. The realization hit her with a shattering force. She thought she knew it all, she was the expert, but all that time something vital had been missing because Faith had never felt like this before.

She had never known what it was to want a man, to want to give him all her heart and soul and body, to need him, to experience the pain of unfulfilled passion and to reach for the ecstasy of a mutual joining. Even with Jess it had not been like this. And she thought suddenly, with shocking clarity, *What was I doing to my life? All that time—what was I doing to my body, my mind?* Faith had thought she had experienced the worst of the regret; she had deliberately cut her losses and banished guilt. But she had never known that somewhere in her future waited a man like Ken. If only she had known... The brief stab of backward pain was bitter.

Ken joked weakly at last, "You may have to drive home." One long-fingered hand rested limply on the steering wheel. He stared at it for a time with patent absorption. Faith's heart beat a slow confined tempo in her ears, and she could not think. She didn't dare try to speak.

Ken took a deep breath, tilting his head back against the seat; he exhaled slowly. "There are," he said softly, still not looking at her, "a million things I want to say to you now," Then he turned his head toward her, his smile slow and tinged with a puzzling sadness. "But you're still not ready to hear them, are you?"

Faith reached for him, her hand falling against his cheek, cupping it, caressing it. She did not know what he meant; she did not know how to answer. She only knew that she wanted this man, this kind and beautiful and gentle man; she wanted to be with him and share with him, and the need was so strong that it blocked out all other emotions, erased all the good and firm and perfectly logical reasons for caution. "Ken," she whispered.

He nuzzled her palm, turning his face to kiss it. His hand came forward to cup the back of her neck, his thumb gently rubbing the corner of her jaw, and the warmth that came slowly into his eyes filled her with happiness as it pushed aside the sadness in his. He smiled at her, and leaned forward to kiss her cheek. "If only you believed as I believe," he said, "this would be much easier."

And his smile turned to a grin of teasing self-mockery as he straightened up, and started the ignition. "I've just got to keep reminding myself we have plenty of time, that's all." He looked at her. "Will you help me fight my most persistent vice, Faith?"

"What—what is it?" Her voice sounded hoarse.

"Impatience," he answered soberly.

"I—don't know if I can, Ken," Faith told him simply, and she caught a flicker of that familiar urgent light in his eyes before he deliberately masked it, and smiled. Ken reached for her hand, and held it all the way back to town.

Chapter Eight

"I have to stop by my office for a minute before we go back to the shop," Ken told her as they reached the outskirts of town. "Do you mind?"

Faith smiled and shook her head automatically, only half-attentive. Like a ray of sunshine parting a foggy day, or a strange but certainly clairvoyant glimpse of the future, a truth had reached out to touch her. She wanted Ken, to be with him, to know him, to explore every possibility his presence in her life offered. She wanted to be a part of his life, to share in that wonderful mystical-magical radiance of purity and purpose he exuded. She wanted to let him teach her how to believe again.

She had been running too long, first escaping from commitment and possible hurt through a decadent, fast-paced life-style, then hiding from the stains of that very life-style by retreating to a small town and shrouding herself with a false image of innocence and simplicity. But now, with Ken, she felt as though she was just beginning to touch something real, something that could finally belong to her, some place she really belonged. Could she afford to let that slip through her fingers?

There were obstacles, she knew. She would have to tell him about Copper Adams. Would he condemn her, as others had, on the basis of the DeFrancis scandal? Would he wonder, as would be surely no more than reasonable, whether or not she still had connections with that underworld and whether the loose ends of her past would one day creep into her present? Or would he simply read between the lines, guessing accurately what kind of woman Copper Adams had been and what kind of life she had led, and would the thought repel him?

Those were chances she would have to take, no more and no less than the simple chances of everyday living. For now, it was enough that she was willing to take them... that Ken was worth it.

Tonight she would ask him to come over for dinner. Just dinner; it was a start. What happened from there would happen. And she had a strong feeling that whatever happened would only be the start of something wonderful.

Faith did not realize where they were until Ken was at her door; she had not even noticed until that moment that the car had stopped. As Ken helped her out it did occur to her to wonder what he meant about stopping by his office—she would have assumed all business was conducted from the halfway house. And then, as she stood on the sidewalk, she experienced a peculiar moment of déjà vu: they were standing in front of the church in which they had first met.

Faith looked around her in some confusion. "What are we doing here?"

Ken chuckled and touched her back lightly to lead her up the walkway. "And I thought I was in bad shape," he murmured dryly. His eyes twinkled at her. "See what these bouts of unfulfilled passion are doing to your mind? You ought to just give in and marry me, it would be a lot healthier—for both of us."

A little thrill of titillating pleasure went through her, despite the fact that Ken's reply made no sense whatsoever. Even the word "passion" when spoken by Ken did something utterly absurd and totally inexplicable to Faith—it made her feel like blushing for no reason at all, it made her fingertips tingle and her pulse speed. Or perhaps it was all due to nothing more than being in his presence.

Ken opened the side door and gestured her down a short carpeted hallway, and still he had not explained what they were doing there. Then he leaned close to her, and his voice was teasing as he murmured in her ear, "Not a word to my secretary about what we were up to parked on the side of the road. She thinks it'll make you go blind." He pushed open the door marked Pastor's Study.

Everything from that point on was to Faith like a film rolled forward in slow motion, frame by stilted frame, and her mind was still one step behind in comprehending it all. She would remember every detail of that small, comfortingly furnished room: the plush beige carpeting, the soft cinnamon-colored sofa and armchair in a coordinating print. The walnut-veneer corner table and the lamp with its burlap shade. The vase of jonquils on the secretary's desk and the smell of coffee. Color-tone file cabinets behind it. The middle-aged woman with her friendly smile and blond French twist. The hum of the typewriter. A picture of the church on one wall, a warm brown-and-gold wheatfield on another. But right then all Faith could see, all she could focus her eyes and her mind and her senses on was the door beyond that desk, and the small black-and-white lettered plate affixed to it that read simply Rev. Kenneth Chapman.

"Hi, Annie." Ken's voice sounded very far away, and it belonged to another man entirely. "Any messages?"

"On your desk, Reverend. How were things at the Crossroads?"

"Running smoothly. Annie, I'd like you to meet a friend of mine, Faith Hilliard. Faith, this is Ann Wilson."

Faith must have said something, and it must have been polite, for the woman's smile widened as she greeted her. She asked if Faith would like some coffee, and Faith must have declined, and then Ken touched her arm lightly and said, "Let me check those messages. It'll just take a minute." And he disappeared behind the door marked Rev. Kenneth Chapman.

That was when everything started to come together for Faith. The Reverend Kenneth Chapman... It repeated itself over again in her head, curiously, wonderingly, like a nursery rhyme or a nonsense word that was repeated simply for its sound or inflection and had

no bearing on the boundaries of logic at all. Reverend Kenneth...Reverend Chapman...Reverend...
He was a minister.

Faith was sitting on the cinnamon sofa, her knees pressed tightly together, her purse clutched in her lap, trying not to look as confused as she felt, trying to push down that awful sense of foreboding that kept stretching its claws inside her stomach. At first all she would consciously acknowledge was surprise, a little bit of shock appropriate to a woman who had just discovered the man she was beginning to fall in love with was not what she had thought. But what had she thought? She hadn't thought at all. Not that it mattered. Not that it made any difference at all...

But it did make a difference. And it was that difference that she refused to think about right now....

The woman at the desk kept giving little smiles and starting up conversations that Faith responded to as best she could, feeling all along that she was being surreptitiously measured and found wanting. There was a lively curiosity in the woman's gaze, a subtle probing to her friendly questions, and of course the entire church must be buzzing with speculation over the woman the minister was seeing....

If only they knew whom the minister was seeing.

Again she tried, not so successfully this time, to shrug away from the thought.

It was too confusing. It was too much and too soon. Moments ago, mere moments, she had reached out and touched hope, a flowering chance for happiness, the beautiful discovery of something good and true in her life at last, and now... Now nothing was the same, nothing made sense, none of it was fair.

It shouldn't have made a difference, but it did. Not to Faith Hilliard, but to Copper Adams. She could no longer avoid that ugly, insistent little knot of certainty forming around her chest and spreading to her stomach, the sense of dread, the unflinching truth. For Copper Adams, with all her excess baggage from the past, did not belong in this man's life. She could, in fact, destroy it.

And it all pummeled her, like cold hard raindrops bent on destruction. What would he say when he knew? As a mere man, he would find it hard enough to accept, but as a minister, responsible for his reputation and his congregation's opinion... how would his congregation react? How long before someone found out? Some astute follower of media events with a sharp memory and an elaborate imagination... it wouldn't take too much investigation, given the right motive, to discover who Faith Hilliard had been before she had moved here two years ago. She could see it now: Local Minister to Marry Mobster's Ex-Girlfriend.

The minister. Faith had a terrifying feeling that she was about to burst into hysterical laughter, and that once she started she wouldn't be able to stop, and she would end up writhing on the floor in helpless convulsions and be carried out on a stretcher, still laughing wildly.

"There, that didn't take long, did it?" Ken came through the door at a cheerful pace, and Faith got to her feet automatically. There he was, in jeans and yellow T-shirt, coming out of the door marked Rev. Ken-

neth Chapman, his thick dark hair catching rays of sunlight from the window, his bright eyes smiling at
her...looking completely out of place and totally at
home here. This was not the same man who had held
her so passionately in his arms only moments ago. This
was not the man who with his lips and his tongue and
his hands had incited her to heights of breathless discovery about herself and her own needs. This was not
the man who had sent her roses and spoke poetry and
had invaded her dreams and her waking yearnings for
the past two weeks...it couldn't be. There was no way
for the two images to fit together. Simply no way.

They were out in the sunlight again. Ken's hand was
resting lightly on Faith's shoulder, and he was saying,
"Since tomorrow's Saturday, it will be the perfect time
for Chelsy to get oriented to the shop. Mickie will drive
her in and pick her up, and I'll try to stop by and help
you out if I get a chance, but I don't think you'll have
any..."

But his words were flowing over Faith like water
over a cliff, and she did not hear anything he said. Why
hadn't he told her, why keep it such a big secret, why
spring it on her now? How could she not have known,
why hadn't anyone said anything? They were passing
the church sign, before which the car was parked, and
one last time it struck her with such clarity that it actually took her breath away, leaping at her in white letters
from a neat black sign shaped like a steeple: Reverend
Kenneth Chapman, Pastor.

Faith had stopped in her steps, and something in her
face must have alerted Ken because he paused as he

reached for the car door. "Faith?" he inquired curiously. "Something wrong?"

"You never told me you were a minister!" she blurted senselessly, breathlessly, and then she just stood there with the words echoing in the still air around them, and somehow the sound of them coming from her own lips made it more real, more believable. She had to accept it. *His name was on the sign, stupid. All this time it's been right here, all you had to do was look... how could you be so stupid?*

For a moment Ken simply stared at her, the sun crinkling his eyes and creasing his forehead as though the explosion of accusation had been in a foreign language and he was having difficulty deciphering it. He said at last, blankly, "What?"

Faith dragged in a breath and it made a little choking sound; she pushed by him quickly toward the car. She was overreacting to this. She was taking it entirely too seriously. She had to settle down and get it sorted out.

But suddenly comprehension seemed to dawn on Ken, and he caught her arm. His face was so close to hers that it broke her heart, and the swift mixture of expressions that crossed his face were both comical and poignant. At first there was incredulity, astonishment, confusion, a hint of amusement and, at last, a small measure of concern. "You're kidding me," he said softly, watching her closely. He saw nothing in her face but confusion and a slowly rising, torturous embarrassment, and his fingers tightened on her arms. "You really didn't know?" he insisted, and the sharp edge of amazement in his voice sounded like amusement.

Faith pulled her arm away and ducked into the car, an ugly, painful color staining her cheeks. She was handling this badly, she knew. The innocence in Ken's eyes was like an accusation to her. How could she have been so stupid? The first man she had fallen for in years, and it had to be a minister.

This would never work. Never.

Ken hesitated a moment and then closed her door. He came slowly around the car to get behind the wheel, and once there he simply sat there, looking at her. "You really didn't know," he said finally. His voice was softened with incredulity, and beneath the wonder in his eyes there was a stunned look, something that resembled the despair that haunted Faith's... as though he had just realized that for all that had passed between them they actually knew nothing about each other, as though he, too, had just been slapped in the face with the truth that all that had been growing between them was nothing more than layers of illusion, and it was a scary thought.

Ken turned away and inserted the key deftly into the ignition. He started to turn it, but then she saw the muscle of his jaw clench, his hands went to the steering wheel and tightened there for a moment, and he said, very lowly, "How could you not know?"

He turned on her, and Faith flinched a little at the sudden flare of anger in his tone. "How could you not know?" he demanded again, incredulously. "Who did you think I was? For goodness' sake, Faith, we met in the church! What did you think I was doing there? Didn't you ever wonder what I did for a living, why I kept such loose hours—why my address, which you so diligently copied down on your order form, happened to be the same address as the pastorium? Didn't you think about me at all?"

The accusation in his voice stung, and she had never before seen that flicker of green ice in his eyes, the tight lines of anger around his mouth. "Of course I wondered!" she cried, and shock and disillusionment were mutating into an angry defense of her own. "But you're the one who never said anything—oh, you made such a big pretense of telling me the story of your life, but you left out one minor little detail, didn't you?" Her voice was growing high, as though it might crack any minute, but there was nothing Faith could do to stop it. Her nails were cutting her palms. "You don't look like a minister," she spat out, "you certainly don't act like one. You never talked about your work—how was I to know?"

"And just what is a minister supposed to look like?" he shot back. "I'm sorry if I don't fit your stereotype, but a uniform didn't exactly come with the job! What was I supposed to do, paste a sign on my forehead?" And then he drew in his breath sharply; he looked at Faith sitting across from him, her color high, her eyes snapping, her fists bunched for self-defense, and something within him seemed to still. Faith saw the slow shadow of regret and self-blame cross his eyes and extinguish the flame of anger that had been there. He turned away, massaging the bridge of his nose with his thumb and his forefinger, and in a moment he said, "I guess you're right." His voice was tired. "Sometimes I don't act much like a minister."

He took another breath and he dropped his hands to

the steering wheel again. "I'm sorry, Faith," he said gently, looking at her. "I didn't mean to shout at you just now, and I certainly never meant to deceive you. I thought you knew, I really did." His eyes went over her face searchingly. Whatever he found there seemed to hurt him, even though he tried to disguise the reaction quickly with a vague smile. "Well," he said softly. And then he lifted an eyebrow, turning back to the steering wheel. He started the ignition. "From the look on your face, I'd say this is going to make a difference between us. We'd better talk about it some more."

But Faith did not know what to say. She was ashamed of herself. She had him apologizing for his vocation as though it were criminal . . . what was she doing? She had no right to do this to him, to act like such a fool over this. She should have known.

They were pulling away from the church, in the direction of her shop. Faith said suddenly, in a small, wondering voice, "That's why—you said—what you did to me that first time we met, when I fell off the stepladder . . . you thought I was the bride!"

A small, tight smile caught the corner of Ken's lips, but he seemed relieved to talk about banalities in the midst of what seemed to be at that moment an overwhelming drama. "I'd never met the bride," he admitted. "Someone pointed her out to me just as she was coming through the door, and you were falling off the ladder and I guess I said the first thing that came to my mind. . . ." He looked at her. His eyes were a very clear green, frighteningly open. "But then I realized I meant it," he said simply.

Faith tried to contain a small shiver, and she edged nearer the door. How could this have happened? How could she have been such a fool? She had known from the first that there was something special about Ken, something that set him apart from other men...she had looked into his eyes and she had known. She had known he was too good for her, nothing about him could ever belong to her.

They stopped in front of the shop, and Ken looked at her for a moment. Faith reached for the door handle.

"I'll help you close up," he decided abruptly, and got out of the car.

It was not quite four-thirty and Faith had no intention of closing up. Work, that was what she needed. She needed to get busily involved in her own life again and give this thing a chance to sink in, and she would think about it later, much later. She didn't think she could handle it now.

Faith turned the Closed sign to Open, and Ken, coming in behind her, immediately flipped it over again. Faith stopped in the middle of the room and turned to him. The expression on her face was helpless, laced with pleading. She didn't want to argue with him again, she didn't want to let him see the smallness within her that had generated her first shock, and she did not want him to suspect the real reason for it. She did not want to see the hurt and disappointment in his eyes again. She only wanted to be left alone, to think this out by herself.

But apparently Ken did not think that was a good idea. He stood there, leaning against the door, watching

her with a sort of weary resignation on his face. And
behind the calmness in his eyes there was a thread of
anxiety, of confusion still, and, yes, of hurt. "So." He
took a firm breath, mustered a crooked smile. "It ap-
pears we have a problem."

Faith turned quickly, going to the cooler to check the
temperature gauge, busily retrieving the watering can
from beneath the counter. "It was just—a surprise,
that's all," she said, forcing lightness into her tone. She
opened a cabinet and took out a bottle of unfluorinated
water. "I mean, I've never known a minster before...
that is, I've known one—them—of course, but I never
had a... was never..." Her cheeks were growing hot-
ter; she was stumbling over her words. She spilled a big
blotch of water onto the papers on the counter as she
filled the watering can. She wanted to bite her tongue.
She couldn't meet his eyes. This was impossible. What
could she say to him, how could she explain to him the
twisting, whirling emotions that were devouring her
now? And beyond it all there was a small biting edge of
anger at him for putting her in this position. It had all
been so perfect, too good to be true. Too good to be
true.

"Relax." There was a lazy smile in Ken's voice, yet
beneath it Faith thought she could sense a sharp edge
of bitterness. "I'm not going to sprout wings and fly
around the room, and I hardly ever embarrass my
friends by breaking into a chorus of 'Ave Maria' at inappropriate times."

Faith cast a quick, despairing look at him, and the
dry mirth in his eyes faded into sympathy. His voice

was gentle, but the question was serious. "I've got to ask you something, Faith," he said. "Is what I'm seeing from you now the same thing that makes ordinary people stop laughing at dirty jokes when I walk into a room and hide their beer cans in flowerpots when I knock on the door...or is it something more? Do you," he asked quietly, "have some religious or moral objection to my ministry?"

"No," she said quickly, her eyes wide and for just that moment completely unshielded. She saw the cautious relief cross his face and then she took the heavy watering can over to the potted plants. "That is," she felt compelled to explain, "I never thought about it...I'm not much of a churchgoer...." Again there was that hysterical bubble of laughter lodged in her throat, and she thought she might choke. Deliberately she squelched it and tried to calm down. She lowered the watering can just as she was on the verge of flooding an African violet, and she looked at him, deliberately, helplessly, resignedly. "I don't know what to say, Ken," she confessed bleakly. "I don't even know what to think." But she did. She knew exactly what was wrong with this picture as the two of them faced each other across the small room crowded with flowers and fragrant with springtime, The Man of God and The Mobster's Woman...

Ken's smile was tender as he crossed the few steps between them. Faith could not move as he took the watering can from her and set it on the shelf, and his hands came up to cup her face very lightly. His eyes were mesmerizing, as soft as velvet yet breathtakingly clear, the warmth of his palms tingled her skin. His scent, as clean as sunshine, drifted over her, and suddenly she was remembering the taste of him, fingers threading through her hair and his body pressing against hers with urgency and demand and the image jarred; she couldn't help it, it frightened her. Ken must have seen it in her eyes because his tone was regretful, almost entreating, as he said softly, "I'm still the same man, Faith."

Was he? Was it possible? Faith pulled her face away, swallowing hard, trying not to look at him. He let his hands drop slowly to his sides, and then, after a moment, he ran one hand through his hair with a heavy breath. "I'm trying to see this from your point of view, Faith," he said, his voice very calm. "But it's hard, because—well, because it's a shock. I never imagined that you were seeing me as anything other than I am, and now—I'm trying to guess how you feel, and it's not easy. So be patient with me, okay?"

He took a few steps away from her, pacing as though to organize his thoughts. He was so beautiful, crossing the room in a spray of sunlight and the shadow of flower petals, moving with grace and control, gold in his hair and the flush of nature on his skin...so gentle, so thoughtful even now, when Faith knew she was hurting him. She did not want to hurt Ken, and everything inside her ached with the disappointment he must be suffering, just as if it were her own. It was her own. Her heart reached out to him, she wanted only to hold him and soothe him, but anything she might do would only hurt him more.

And it would hurt her. She couldn't go through it again, having her life spread out for all the world to see and judge—for Ken, this good and innocent man, to see and judge. She had tried so hard to escape from it all, the humiliation, the pain, the guilt, simply to put it behind her and forget. But mistakes from the past were never completely put behind. They were always there, hiding around the corner, waiting to spring out and attack when they were least expected.

If only they had never met! If only he had remained just another stranger who passed her shop day after day without her ever having known of his existence.

He stopped in the middle of the floor, turning to her with palms spread, a quirky little smile haunting his face and making him look suddenly very vulnerable. "So help me out, Faith," he entreated. "What are you thinking?"

How could she tell him, what could she say to him? Despair bubbled up inside her, feeding a turmoil of hopelessness, and it was so unfair. How could she do this to him? "Ken," she blurted somewhat desperately, "this—this isn't going to work." She saw the quick flash of denial in his eyes, and she sought quickly for some way to make him see the logic of it, struggling to put it into words. "You're—not like other men, Ken," she said, and her eyes pleaded for his silence as she tried to get through this, tried to make him see. "This is not a game—you can't afford to make mistakes. People are watching you, Ken, depending on you ... for some sort of ... of—" she groped for words "—moral example.... You know it's true. You can't just—"

And slowly the alarm that had been in his face faded to gentle relief. "Is that it, then?" He took a step toward her. "Is that what's bothering you?" The soft light in his eyes, tinged just slightly now with that familiar hint of amusement, seemed to reach out and embrace her. Soon, Faith knew, his arms would follow. She quickly picked up the watering can again and he stopped, acknowledging her signal with a sigh. "Darling," he said patiently, "my congregation knows I'm unmarried. They also don't expect me to stay that way forever. I'm allowed a social life with all the accepted trappings of courtship and wooing. How else," he teased, "am I ever going to find the right woman and settle down to become a proper family man?" Faith spilled a liberal portion of water onto the plant stand; it dripped with a slow dull plopping sound onto the floor. "And Faith," he said quietly, very seriously, "this is no mistake. I'm not taking any risks."

Faith shook her head violently, but no words would come. There was an awful burning in her throat and her chest ached. She heard Ken's long, heavy breath behind her, and that, mixed with the muted drip of water on the floor, was the only sound.

Why did she care so much? How had she gotten so involved with him? It shouldn't matter; another time, with another man, it wouldn't have. But with Ken, for whom she had come to care far too much and far too quickly, it made all the difference in the world.

And then she heard him cross the room toward her. He had gripped the watering can and replaced it firmly on the shelf before she knew what he was doing, and then, before she could even gasp with surprise, he was lifting her by the waist and setting her down securely on the counter. His face was grim, set with determination. "All right, Faith," he said, "let's get this out in the open."

He took both of her hands in a strong clasp and held them firmly. His face was open yet stubborn, lined with a trace of intractability, his eyes deep and intense and compelling, completely devoid of apology or reticence. "Yes," he said quietly, "I am different from other men. It was both a choice I made and a choice that was never mine to make—it's what I am and I'm not ashamed of it. Yes, my life revolves around a personal and very intense relationship with my God, and yes, I give Him my first devotion. I have a firm and unshakable belief in the mighty and mystical powers outside myself and higher than myself, and I will not compromise my convictions for anyone or anything." He took a breath, watching her, studying her with both caution and courage, waiting for her to object, but Faith could do nothing, could say nothing. She just sat there with the grip of his hands instilling all of the wonder that was this man into her, and she was aching inside, falling apart inside. She wanted to cry, she wanted to scream and beat her fists against him and rail against the unfairness of it all. She wanted to hold him and never let him go.

The tight swelling in her chest pushed its way upward, scorching her throat, burning her eyes. Ken saw it, and his face softened. He released one of her hands to stroke her cheek lightly. "But darling," he said softly, "I am just a man. I'm not a prophet, not immortal, not untouchable. Very human." His tender smile tried to tease a response from her. "As preachers go, I don't even fit the mold very well—as I believe you pointed out to me not long ago. I mean, I run around in tennis shorts and Izod shirts. I listen to rock music. I get my hair styled. I even," he confided with a coaxing twinkle in his eye, "read Harold Robbins and Erica Jong late at night, when everyone else in town has gone to bed, and enjoy every lascivious word." The teasing in his smile faded to seriousness, and he said, "I'm just a man trying to serve his calling in the best way he knows how—by making the life we lead here on earth a little easier, a little richer, a little more fulfilling for as many people as I can. My congregation has learned to accept me, as unorthodox and noncomformist as I am, imperfections and idiosyncrasies included," he finished simply, and the look he gave her was searching and questioning. "Can you?"

Faith looked at him, all the torment and the helplessness she felt crowding up her throat, twisting in her eyes, burning and blurring her vision. She felt his hand stroke her face, his eyes examining hers intensely, trying to read the secrets there, and then she felt the tight, encouraging grip of both his hands on hers again, and all she could do was shake her head. "It's not—that," she managed thickly. The effort it took for her to speak, actually to meet his eyes, took more courage than Faith was aware she possessed. "I—I think you're wonderful, Ken, I really do..." He squeezed her hands briefly, and then she thought she wouldn't be able to go on. She tried very hard to keep her voice steady. "It's...not a matter of...conflict of faiths, or anything, it's not that I...don't respect your work. But I...don't think... It's just that—"

"That you're intimidated by me again," he supplied quietly, and when Faith met his eyes there was no accusation there, no anger. Only understanding. And his sincerity probed right into her mind, opening and penetrating carefully guarded layers of her, insisting that she accept, making her want to believe. "Don't do that, Faith," he commanded quietly. "Don't do that to yourself, or us. You're thinking you're not good enough for me and it's insane, it's dangerous." His hands were slowly tightening on hers again, demanding attention, drawing acceptance. "Don't you know," he insisted with low intensity, "what there is in you that attracts me? I can see it there, even if you can't. Don't ever say you're not good enough, because it's really the other way around."

Faith closed her eyes slowly. Oh, how she wanted to believe him. How she wanted to melt into his arms and embrace all that he offered...how she wished it could be.

She took a thick, uneven breath. Again she shook her head, violently. Her voice, with all the force she could put behind it, was still little more than a broken whisper. "You don't even know me, Ken!"

He was silent for a moment. His finger touched her cheek, stroked her wet lashes lightly. "Open your eyes, darling," he commanded gently. "Look at me."

Faith valiantly fought to keep the tears from spilling

over as she obeyed. Her one remaining hand clenched convulsively in her lap, and his still covered it comfortingly. "I know," he told her quietly, his unashamed sincerity penetrating the very fibers of her heart, "all I need to know about you. I knew that from the very first moment I saw you, and everything I've learned since has been nothing but icing on the cake." And then, endearingly, with a half-smile that tore at her heart, he brushed a finger over her eyelid again and suggested, "Don't cry. Please?"

Faith caught a breath that threatened to turn into a sob, and she deliberately forced the corners of her mouth upward, blinking back the tears. How did it happen that this man had come into her life, how did she deserve him, and how could she bear to hurt him anymore...?

"Better," he smiled, and dropped his hand to hers again. In a moment the smile faded into seriousness. "Look," he said simply. "I realize that it must be—a special thing for a woman to become involved with a minister. She probably has to think about things she wouldn't with another man. There's the fact that she will always be considered a—kind of extension of her husband, married to the church as well as to him. Certain things will be expected of her that wouldn't be under ordinary circumstances. She has to resign herself to the fact that she will constantly have to take a backseat to his ministry, and even to his faith. You're right—we're always being watched, expected to set an example...and I'm not saying it's easy. When I went into the ministry I wasn't prepared for it, and sometimes I still have a hard time dealing with it, and I know it's a lot to ask of anyone." His lips tightened wryly with a slight tilt of his head. "And it's hard for me to relate to this now because I thought all this time you were thinking about those things, and accepting them, and it turns out I'm springing this all on you at once, and I know it's not fair. You have some adjusting to do. You need some time to get used to it. That's fine." He slowly released her hands; the smile he gave her was not as confident as it was brave. "We'll take it easy for a while; I'll give you some time to think. Is that fair?"

Faith had to swallow, twice, before she could make herself smile. Why didn't she tell him now? Why prolong this agony, why hold on to false hope? Because she wanted to, that was all. Hope had begun to awaken and stir in Faith the moment Ken Chapman walked into her life, and she wanted to hold on to it as long as she could.

Still, she couldn't believe what she said next.

"Yes," she said, a little huskily. "That's fair."

Relief slowly relaxed lines of tension on his face that Faith had not even been aware were there. An easy twinkle sparkled in his eyes as he placed one affectionate finger under her chin. "Care to come to services with me Sunday?" he invited. "I'll do my special fire-and-brimstone number just for you. You'll be so impressed you won't even consider letting me get away."

Incredibly, Faith heard a small bubble of laughter issuing from her own throat. "I think I'll have to work up to that," she said.

He smiled. The smile lingered on his lips, in his eyes,

fell over her and caressed her and wrapped itself around her heart. "Okay," he said. His hand nestled itself around her face, his thumb rubbed with slow affection against her chin. "You think about it, and while you're thinking..." He leaned forward and kissed her cheek sweetly, adoringly. His voice was very soft. "Try to remember to believe in miracles, huh?"

It wasn't until he was out of the shop that Faith started to cry.

Chapter Nine

Faith did not see Ken that next week at all. Chelsy told her that Ken was conducting a series of special services directed at the young people of the community during that week and grumbled every night because she was required to attend. It turned out, of course, that no one was forcing Chelsy to attend anything, and her complaining was nothing more than an attempt to disguise her pride in the fact that she had been chosen as an usherette.

Chelsy's presence in the shop was a surprising and sometimes delightful experience for Faith, and the novelty helped occupy her thoughts and get her over the shock of adjustment to and the absence of Ken. Ken knew his business when it came to matching his protégées to a job, and beneath Chelsy's obstreperous attitude was a thinly hidden streak of genuine creative talent and a pride in her sense of accomplishment that was bubbling to get through the layers of defensiveness she had built over the years.

She was happiest when putting together arrangements and bouquets, and some of her creations were simply stunning. Faith gave her every opportunity to indulge that talent, and within a matter of days was gratified to see Chelsy begin to open up, to forget her street language and her sullen expression, and actually to glow in response to a compliment. The girl was a quick learner, too, and had a head for figures and, to Faith's absolute astonishment, a way with customers.

The people who came into Faith's shop were at first curious, then amused and at last totally helpless beneath the nonstop chatter of the miniskirted, gum-chewing teenager in two pounds of makeup who could, in no time flat and leaving absolutely no room for argument, convince them that daisies at seven dollars a bouquet were tacky and passé and that sweetheart roses at only twice the price would make a far more appropriate gift. Sometimes Faith had to hide in the back room, doubled over with silent laughter, while Chelsy recited, perfectly deadpan, an imaginary list of allergies and communicable diseases attributed to some of the less expensive varieties of flower while extolling the virtues of the most expensive bouquet they sold... or while shamelessly coming on to a teenage boy until he had spent every cent he had in the shop, and then cutting him dead. The free enterprise system had been designed exclusively with Chelsy Warren in mind.

By the middle of the week, Chelsy was making deliveries on her own, and Faith had decided to raise her salary to two dollars an hour. She wished she could pay her a regular salary, but she did not feel free to do that without consulting Ken first, and Ken was making himself very scarce in her life these days.

He called every day, but the telephone calls never lasted more than thirty seconds. Certainly he was busy with the special services he was conducting that week, but Faith knew he could have taken a few minutes to stop by the shop, and he had to eat lunch. She also knew that he was being very literal about giving her time to think it over.

Faith was doing a good job of not thinking about anything until she came into the shop on Tuesday afternoon and saw one of her own slim white florist boxes, tied with a red ribbon, lying on the countertop. Chelsy had been minding the shop while Faith attended to some banking and other personal business, and Faith assumed that Chelsy had started packaging up orders while she was away. She started to put the box in the refrigerator where it belonged until delivery time, and Chelsy said, coming in from the back room just then, "Don't look at me. I told him not to leave it lying out on the counter—there was no telling when you'd be back."

Faith inquired curiously, "Who?"

Chelsy said, opening the storage cabinet for more florist's wire, "Reverend Ken. He told me to just leave it there, that you'd know what to do with it." And Chelsy disappeared into the back room again.

Faith slipped the ribbon away and opened the box with fingers that were somewhat unsteady. Inside, nestled in tissue paper, was one of her best long-stemmed red roses. Faith felt the breath leave her body in a single slow rush, and she picked up the card uncertainly. "A single red rose," he had written, "for passion."

Faith looked at the card for a long time, and the melting feeling that had started in the center of her chest spread slowly outward along the course of her arms and her legs and upward to the roots of her hair, like an injection of something warm and tingling beneath her skin. She closed her eyes and let it fill her. How was she supposed to fight this? What did he think she was made of—iron?

Chelsy poked her head through the door again. "He also said to change his order from pink to red," she remembered, and frowned a little. "I thought he meant flowers for the church, but I looked in the file and I couldn't find the order. Do you know what he was talking about?"

Faith folded the card slowly and put it back on the box, replacing the lid. "Yes," she told Chelsy quietly. "I know what he was talking about." He was talking about devotion and understanding and constancy, hope that flowered into passion and passion that grew into... what? He was talking about something deep and abiding and real, something that went beyond the borders of everyday encounters and touched the very edges of the soul. This was the man whose eyes could see into the depths of the heart and find only beauty there, a man who could cry over the loss of one wayward child, a man who spoke the language of flowers.... And what did he want from her? What did she have to offer him?

And how could she tell him?

"ALL RIGHT, LANCE, let's put all our cards on the table. Let's get a good look at this thing." Five hours later

Faith was pacing the length of her small living room, her hands folded and pressed into the point of her chin, her brow knit with concentration. Lance was sitting on the coffee table, contentedly licking up a bowl of soup that Faith had not touched. Beside him, in a slim milk-glass vase, stood a single red rose.

"First," she said, turning with a slow, decisive breath, "I guess I have to admit to myself that this man is for real. He's probably the most real thing that has ever happened to me . . . maybe the only real thing. And he wants me." Her voice fell slightly, and the mixture was both of wonder and despair. "For some crazy, indefinable reason he wants me. But he doesn't even know me," she said, and her hands tightened with the fierceness in her voice. "What's going to happen when he finds out who I really am?"

Then why don't you tell him, the cat's implacable, yellow-eyed stare seemed to taunt. *Tell him and get it over with.*

Faith took a short breath, turning toward the window and away from the challenge. "I mean," she continued to herself reasonably, "all else being equal, it's obvious he's not in a position to engage in short-term relationships, and how do I know I even want the kind of life he could offer on a permanent basis? What kind of minister's wife would I make?"

She tried to laugh but couldn't quite manage it. And a little voice answered, *What kind of minister does Ken make? Don't try to stereotype his life, Faith, or yours with him, because it just won't work.* No, there would be nothing traditional or boring about life with Ken, no matter what the trappings of his vocation dictated. He was a man of his own realm, outside the bonds of rules made by mortals, and whatever the future might hold with him it would be neither quiet nor predictable.

She rubbed her temples wearily, trying to press away the distracting logic. "It could destroy him," she whispered, and lifted her eyes to stare blankly at the opposite wall. "Not only his career, but his faith in his own judgment and his belief in people and his innocence...his whole life." How could she do that to him? How could she tell him and see that gentleness in his clear green eyes darken to disgust and mist with reproach and disbelief and haze with the dull bitterness of disillusionment? How could she do that to Ken, who had brought her nothing but happiness, who had opened the door for her to believe in miracles, who had awakened her to the possibilities of life she had never before dreamed of...how could she destroy the man who, by his very existence, had opened up the festering corners of her soul and cleansed them with sunlight? How could she tell him?

But did she have any right to go on offering him an illusion, the fantasy he wanted to see...just as she had done for those other men, the shallow, vain and hardened men whose only fantasy was to believe, if only for one night, that the glamorous Copper Adams belonged to them?

Faith brought her hands up to cover her face with a deep, dragged-in breath that was meant to instill courage; it was in fact only a violent turning away from remembered shame. What was she going to do?

Lancelot sprang silently from the table to the sofa and sat there, watching her, licking his paws.

"I'm not that woman anymore," Faith said fiercely, and her hands came down to lace tightly together once again under her chin. "I'm not." That was never a real part of her, it was just a game she played while she was in the grip of an illness that was as real as hepatitis or Asian flu. It had left its scars, no doubt, but they were the consequences she had to deal with, and even they would disappear in time. Was a person to be held accountable for actions committed in the height of delirium, was a patient blamed for getting sick? No, she had to put it all behind her because it had nothing to do with the person she was now. The woman she was now was no more than exactly what Ken saw in her...the owner of a small-town business, the daughter of loving parents, a spinster who talked to her cat and had peanut butter and pickles for dinner and was too concerned about hurting people's feelings to even fire a disastrous employee...a woman who had been through some trauma in her life and was just a little bit afraid of trying a relationship...a vulnerable, pliable, very lonely woman who needed him more, much more, than she would admit.

And what it all boiled down to was, "If I tell him, I'll lose him," she said out loud, very softly. Did she really want to lose Ken?

And then, sneaking out of nowhere, a small voice whispered, *If you don't tell him, who will?*

Faith looked very steadily at Lancelot, who was busily immersed in his bath. Very few men could forgive a background like hers in the woman he wanted to call his own.

Of course, Ken was no ordinary man. But did she really want to take the chance?

Faith thought about it. How could her past hurt Ken if he never knew about it? Was there any reason for him to know? What good would telling him do?

He'll find out, another vicious little voice whispered. *Your face was plastered on every magazine cover of any repute for almost three years, for goodness' sake, not to mention the media coverage with DeFrancis... who are you trying to kid? It's only a matter of time.*

But maybe time was all she needed. Time to let the relationship grow, to find strength, to convince him that she was never really the wicked moll the papers had made her out to be, and even if she was, she had changed. Just a little time, that was all she was asking for.

And could she really offer herself to this good and perfect man on false pretenses? What kind of relationship could they have with a secret such as that lying between them?

Faith had put the past behind her. It never rose to haunt her anymore... or at least it never had, until Ken had come into her life. No one else in her new life knew what her old life had been. Why should she suddenly let it become part of the present again? It was over, done with, forgotten. It had nothing to do with her and Ken now. If only she could go on believing that.

She looked at Lancelot helplessly. What was she going to do?

But she knew, she had known all along what she was going to do. As with Ken's ministry, it was both a choice she made and a choice that was never hers to make. She was going to follow her heart, because—"I love him, Lance," she said out loud, and the force of that final admission shook a shiver from her. She clasped her arms across her chest to contain it; she bowed her head hopelessly and let it fill her, opening her eyes at last to a truth that was so overwhelming it made her weak. "God help me," she whispered, "I love him."

IF NOTHING ELSE GOOD resulted from the traumatic events of that spring, the discovery of Chelsy would almost have made up for it all. Aside from the fact that Faith had never had a more efficient assistant in her life, the girl in herself was a fascination, half-child, half-woman, who was far tougher and much smarter than she had any right to be; watching the layers unfold, bit by bit, behind which the true Chelsy lay hidden was a source of constant and almost obsessive interest to Faith.

At first the girl was defensive about everything, not overtly uncooperative, but never losing an opportunity to grumble and complain and **curs**e about everything—from the Crossroads, which had given her a second chance; to her parents, on whom she blamed everything, from inflation to her mousy brown hair; to the hokey little town, and the people who walked its streets. Faith was of the firm and somewhat amused conviction that the girl could have been handed the keys to a brand-new Mercedes and she would have only scowled and said, "What the hell kind of crap is this?"

Once when Faith was browsing in a dime store she returned with a small blue Smurf doll with the nameplate "Grouchy" attached to its base and placed it in a prominent location on the corner of the worktable Chelsy had claimed for her own. Not a word was ever said about the doll, but several times during that day Faith caught Chelsy trying to suppress a grin, and when Chelsy left that evening a small blue plastic face was peeking out of the back pocket of her jeans. Faith noticed a slow but definite improvement in her attitude from then on.

Chelsy was by no means an uncommunicative girl— as evidenced by her approach to the customers—but it took a great deal of perception to see through the bravado she spun out and get to the core of the truth. Faith was most gratified when, as time went on, those glimpses of truth came more and more frequently, and voluntarily.

At first Chelsy tried to impress Faith with recitations of her life on the streets. She told about turning tricks for ten dollars a shot and making a small fortune selling acid and cocaine that she had stolen from a pimp, and even though Faith, as experienced a judge of character as she was, doubted very seriously that the girl had ever done any of those things, the casual ease with which Chelsy tossed off those stories made her blanch. The young girl did not know how close she had been to falling into that life, and she had no idea what a hell it could really be. Faith did not want to see that happen to Chelsy. She desperately did not want to see it.

On Friday afternoon Faith said casually, "What do you say we close up early this afternoon? With the business we've done this week, we can afford it. Besides, it's Friday. We ought to celebrate."

Chelsy looked briefly gratified, as she always did whenever Faith referred to their conduct of business in the plural. But then she shrugged. "You go ahead," she said. "I have to wait here anyway till Mrs. Allen picks me up at five-thirty. Then—" she grimaced "—I have to go to church."

Faith thought for a minute. "What if I call Mrs. Allen and check it out with her, then we can go have a pizza or something. I'll drop you off at church afterward."

Chelsy looked at her suspiciously. "What for?" Somewhere along the road Chelsy had learned that nothing in life was free, and every kindness was to be regarded as a Trojan horse. It wasn't a bad lesson to learn, but Chelsy had learned it far too early.

"Fringe benefits," Faith told her, and then grinned. "Come on, kid, give me a break. You've made me a rich woman this week—let me splurge!"

Chelsy maintained the skeptical look a moment longer, but she could not hide the childlike pride in her eyes. It tugged at Faith's heart to think that anyone should be that badly deprived of praise and a sense of accomplishment, and though she was trying not to spread it on too thick, Chelsy deserved every compliment she got.

"You don't mind if we stop here first, do you?" Faith said as she pulled the van into her own driveway. "I have to feed my cat."

"Nah, I don't mind." Chelsy pretended lack of interest as she climbed down out of the van and followed Faith inside at a lazy pace, but her eyes were busily taking in every detail.

Chelsy jumped back, frightened, as Lancelot greeted her with a great show of hissing, spitting and threatening swipes of the paw, and Faith tossed over her shoulder, "Don't mind him. He won't let anyone near him except me, and I think that's only because I feed him." And Ken, Faith remembered with a pang as she sat the bowl of cat food on the floor. But then, Ken was very special.

"Come on back here for a minute," Faith invited on her way to the bedroom. "I just want to freshen up my makeup."

"You never wear makeup," the astute young girl pointed out, and Faith tried to suppress a grin. It wasn't easy putting anything over on this one.

"Special occasion," Faith replied, and sat down at her dressing table, drawing out a huge box filled with all the chemicals and potions of her past.

"Wow," Chelsy breathed when Faith opened it. "What'd you do, rip off the whole cosmetic counter at Saks, or something?"

Faith laughed, shaking a bottle of creamy foundation. "Close," she replied. "I had some friends in the cosmetic business," she said, and it was not entirely a lie. She had done lots of shoots for cosmetics ads. "I picked up a few tricks."

Chelsy settled on the edge of the bed and watched as Faith cleansed her face thoroughly with witch hazel and applied moisturizer, inquiring, "What's that for?"

"It makes the foundation go on smoother," Faith answered, and inside she felt the smug satisfaction of a well-executed plan. The girl was hooked.

"Hot date tonight?" Chelsy inquired after a moment, uncapping a container of gold eye glitter.

Faith smiled, noticing in the mirror the way the girl carefully observed Faith's technique of highlighting her brow bones. "You never can tell."

"So." Chelsy picked up an eyebrow pencil. "You going to marry Reverend Ken, or what?"

Faith smudged her eyeliner and quickly wiped it off. She tried to keep her voice steady. "What makes you ask that, Chelsy?"

Chelsy shrugged, opening a palette of pale eye shadow. "He's not such a bad guy, for a preacher. Cute-looking, too. He's got a good way of talking to you...like he's been where you're at, or something. Doesn't give you any hype. I don't mind him," she decided. "I guess I really don't mind him at all. This is a pretty color." She ran her finger across the edge of a pastel green shadow.

"It would look good with your eyes," Faith said. "Would you like to try it?" She was watching Chelsy in the mirror, but her mind was going over what the girl had said, lingering and clinging to any words spoken about Ken as though the mere thought of him could conjure up his presence. Somehow the simple words of praise from this young girl told her more about Ken than anything else had ever done, and something within Faith tightened and swelled with it.

Soon Chelsy was sitting in front of the mirror, her young face stripped bare, while Faith showed her how to highlight her eyes with pale green shadow in the outer corners and sand pink on the lid, how to make her eyes look wider with a single stroke of a separating mascara brush. She watched with patient absorption as Faith restructured her cheekbones with a contour pencil and an almost transparent rose blush, narrowed her nose with cover stick, and let the natural color of her lips shine through a barely tinted gloss. Soon, wide-eyed at her own reflection, Chelsy was trying out new hairstyles, pushing her hair up and to the side, and was amazed and then delighted when Faith volunteered to French-braid it. Less than an hour later there stood before Faith a girl she hardly recognized—fragile and pretty, with her hair pulled in an elegant braid away from a face that was clean and delicately colored, Chelsy the way she was meant to be.

"Wow," said Chelsy, staring into the mirror with a wide-eyed mixture of disbelief and apprecation. "I look weird."

Faith laughed. "You look terrific," she corrected.

And, to Faith's great amazement, Chelsy actually began to smile. "Yeah," she admitted. "I guess I do, kind of." But then she stepped back and looked critically in the mirror at her striped sweatshirt, purple miniskirt and cowboy boots. "Except for this getup," she acknowledged, adding, "Weird."

Faith thought for only a moment. "Do you want to try on something of mine?"

Chelsy gave her a cynical look. "What is this, dress-up time or something?"

Faith shrugged and closed the makeup box, but Chelsy wandered over to her closet. "Will you look at this?" the girl murmured after a moment. "Where'd you get all these fancy threads?" She pulled out a simple white shirtwaist. "What is this, real silk?" She shot Faith another skeptical look. "Why don't you ever wear anything like this to work?"

Faith laughed. She did not tell Chelsy that she hadn't worn any of the clothes on that side of the closet for over two years and probably never would again. "And wreck them with plant food and fertilizer? Look at the label," she tempted.

Chelsy did, and let out a low breath. "Ralph Lauren, are you kidding me? This must have cost a fortune."

"Try it on," Faith invited.

Chelsy looked at her for one more disbelieving moment, but it was obvious she wasn't about to turn her back on that kind of offer. The dress wasn't a perfect fit—Chelsy was much larger in the bust than Faith was, a fact that they both laughed over—but the dress had been designed when hemlines were shorter, and fashion now compensated for the two inches' difference in their heights. And when Faith found a pair of white medium-heeled sandals that fit Chelsy, the young girl's transformation was complete. She looked as if she had been born to the style.

"If the kids could see me now," Chelsy murmured into the mirror wonderingly.

"Wear it tonight," Faith volunteered generously. "It looks great on you. Give everybody a thrill."

Chelsy laughed and for a moment looked reluctant, but the temptation was obviously too great to resist. "I'll take good care of it," she promised. "I'll make Mrs. Allen put it in one of those dry-cleaning bags tonight and bring it back to you in the morning."

Faith smiled dismissingly, and then a sudden thought occurred to her. She went over to the dresser and opened a drawer, pulling out a gold pendant with a heart-shaped filigree woven around a single pearl. "This looks great with it," she said, and came to fasten the necklace around Chelsy's neck. "The pearl is a little dull—they get that way if you don't wear them, you know—but if you rub it against the silk for a few minutes it will shine right up. There." She stepped back to admire her handiwork. "Perfect."

"Hey, wait a minute." Chelsy carefully lifted the pendant in her hand. "This looks expensive—real gold and everything. I can't wear this. What if I lost it?"

Faith shook her head and smiled. "No, it's yours to keep. Someone gave it to me." It had been a graduation gift from her father, but the wide light in Chelsy's eyes made Faith want suddenly nothing more than to give it to the young girl. "I'm allergic to gold, so I can't wear it," she quickly added as she saw reluctance clouding in Chelsy's face. "Consider it a token of my appreciation for a job well done."

"Oh," Chelsy said softly, lowering her eyes again to the necklace. "Wow." She looked at the expensive trinket for a long time, and it struck Faith suddenly that she was trying not to cry. Was this the only kindness anyone had ever shown the girl? What had happened to her at such a young age to make her so hard, so reluctant to trust good intentions, so surprised when something nice happened to her? Faith wished intently that she had made the gesture much earlier, that she had been around to remind Chelsy of her own worth when it had really mattered. And she hoped it was not now too late....

Chelsy looked up suddenly, and there was such a look of desperation in her eyes that Faith was startled. "Miss Hilliard," she said quickly, "I have to tell you—" But then she broke off. Faith could see the struggle working in Chelsy's face, and she wanted to make it easier but she didn't know how.

"Chelsy?" she prompted.

Chelsy lowered her eyes. "Nothing," she mumbled. "It wasn't anything. Just—thanks for the necklace, that's all."

They went out for pizza, and, as proof of the adage that the clothes make the man—or woman—Chelsy was delightful company. She chatted about school, which wasn't so bad now that she only went half a day, and about life at the Crossroads, and even began to open up a little about her parents. Throughout the meal Faith noticed that her hand kept wandering up to fondle the necklace, and the gesture touched Faith, making her feel warm inside. Making her smile.

Faith stopped the van in front of the church at a quarter of seven. The parking lot was full, and the street was lined with cars; people were walking up the sidewalk and lingering on the lawn. Before her the illuminated sign read: Reverend Kenneth Chapman, Pastor. Faith felt a catch in her heart.

"Aren't you coming?" Chelsy said when Faith made no move to get out.

Faith was embarrassed to tell the girl she had never had any intention of attending the service. She was afraid her reluctance might diminish her in Chelsy's eyes somehow. After all, Faith was a friend of Ken's, how could she admit she had never attended one of his services? What kind of example was that setting for Chelsy—for everyone who knew, or might yet know, about her relationship with Ken? Those grim complications Faith had tried to avoid thinking about were already surfacing.

"Come on," persuaded Chelsy. "It's not all that bad. I mean, he's not boring or anything. You might even like it." She grinned self-consciously. "Sometimes I do."

Faith managed an almost convincing smile. "You go ahead. There are some things I want to do first."

"I'll save you a good seat," Chelsy promised, and jumped gracefully down from the van.

Faith waited until the girl went inside before driving away.

Thirty minutes later Faith was parked again in front of the church, feeling ashamed, cowardly and very uncomfortable. This was the man she loved, and she was deliberately avoiding sharing the most important part of his life. She had, that entire past week, avoided even thinking about it. In all her cautious imaginings, in all her conscious logic, she had never been able to

envision herself sitting in a church pew while Ken
looked down at her from the pulpit. Did she think that
seeing him there now, hearing him do what he was
called to do, would paint too graphic a picture of what
he was and what she was? Might it finally become
real?

If so, then the most important thing she had ever
done in her life would be to walk into that building and
take a seat.

Faith's palms were sweaty and her mouth was dry.
She kept trying to picture Ken, wearing the robes of his
profession, looming above her in the performance of
his duty. He would be a stranger to her. But he would
be the stranger she had fallen in love with. . . .

So what are you afraid of? she chided herself angrily.
That you'll be struck by lightning if you go inside?

Faith got out of the van and slammed the door hard.

The small church had been almost empty the last
time she was there. Now it was full to capacity, and not
only with teenagers, she noticed, but with men and
women of all ages. There were a couple of men in suits
standing by the door, their attention fixed on the front
of the auditorium, but Faith smiled weakly at them and
shook her head when they offered to find a seat for her.
Above the pounding of her heart she could hear Ken's
microphoned voice. She crept inside the foyer and
stood near the end of the last row of pews, by the door.
The service was almost over.

Ken was wearing a sports coat over a beige turtleneck
sweater, and he was not in the pulpit. Even as Faith
entered, he had detached the microphone from its

stand and was coming easily down the steps as he spoke, toward the front of the church. The bright overhead lights flickered on his hair and seemed to trace his vibrant body with a kind of hazy aura. Faith caught her breath, because he had never looked more beautiful to her.

"So maybe it's not as bad as you think," Ken said. He had reached the front of the building and now half-sat casually upon the edge of the altar table that held an arrangement of flowers that someone had ordered from Faith's shop only that week. He was talking easily, matter-of-factly, just as though he were addressing one of the kids out at the Crossroads in a private conversation, giving no thought to the fact that he was affecting the life of almost two hundred men, women and children.

"You all know the story about the woman a whole town wanted to stone, don't you?" Ken continued conversationally. "She was the town whore—" And he lifted one endearing eyebrow. "I can say that word," he assured his audience, "it's in the Bible—and a bunch of jealous wives and outraged husbands, most of whom you can bet had been at her hut the Saturday night before—" there was an appreciative titter "—got together and decided they had had enough of this vice and corruption in their fine town, and it was time to put a stop to it. They were going to make an example of her. What they really needed, of course, was a scapegoat."

Faith closed her eyes and a smile of sweet, weary resignation played with her lips. She should have known that on this night of all nights Ken would choose that particular parable to tell.

"Well, Jesus came along right about then, and you can bet those folks must have been pretty embarrassed to have a stranger interrupt their noble proceedings, but when he saw what was going on, all he said was, 'Let him who is without sin among you be the first to throw a stone at her.' And you know what? One by one every one of those fine townspeople walked away. It makes you wonder, sometimes, doesn't it, what kind of secrets they were hiding?

"So you're looking at me, and you're saying, what does this guy know about my troubles? I don't need some dude in a fancy suit passing judgment on me... and let me tell you something, kids, neither do I. There's not a person in this room who can afford to have their lives examined too closely, and I'll be the first one to jump up and say so. Because ten years ago, you know where I was?" His bright eyes traveled around the room, touching and arresting each face before him. Faith felt herself yearning toward him, reaching and connecting with him, and for a moment it was as though he stood there and spoke for no one else but her. "I was sitting in a county jail charged with driving a stolen car and possession of amphetamines." During a very slight pause his lips curved into a slight, reminiscent smile. "And you know what else? That was small potatoes compared to some of the stuff I had really done—that just happened to be the one time I got caught. Oh, yes, I was a real hell-raiser. Of course you'd never know it to look at me now." He said it so easily, and a small wink from him drew another nervous rustle of laughter from the crowd. He sobered again. "I experimented with drugs, I had knife fights, I was well on my way to becoming an alcoholic at nineteen. My favorite pastime was wrecking the cars my dad kept buying me. The only way I got through college was to cheat on every major exam. And it gets better. You think you're bad? There's nothing any of you out there have done or thought about doing that I haven't done, and you know what else? I did it for fun. No heavy psychological reasons, no deep-hidden motivations—I did it because I wanted to, no excuses, no apologies. Sure, I got what I deserved, and I knew it even then— but I also knew something else."

Once again his eyes traveled over the audience one by one, gently riveting them to heightened attention. Faith held her breath lest those eyes fall on her, but if they did he gave no sign of it. "I served six months of a two-year sentence," he said quietly, "because I had a good lawyer and parents who never gave up on me. And I figured out one thing real quick: there had to be a better way to live. The things I saw in that time, the things I did, and the things that happened to me would turn your stomach. If you want to hear about them, come see me, I'll tell you. But I'll tell you one thing right now: I don't want that to ever happen to you. Not any of you.

"Listen," he said, and he leaned forward a little, the intensity in his eyes drawing like a calm and welcoming beacon, "have you got problems? You got a habit you can't kick or some girl in trouble or just a plain bad feeling? Come talk to me about it. Come see me or one of the counselors and let us see if we can't help you work it out. Do you think we're going to leak the information to your parents or the cops?" He shook his head slowly. "It's just between us. We may not have all the answers, but we can help you find some pretty important ones, and that's what we're here for—to help."

Faith turned and slipped silently out the door. There were tears on her cheeks when the balmy night air brushed across her face, and she loved him more than ever.

Chapter Ten

It was nine o'clock the next evening, Saturday, when Faith saw Ken Chapman again. It was so much like the first time he had appeared on her doorstep that it was eerie, as though Fate had come full circle. Lance had left a half hour ago for his nightly prowl around town. Faith had just gotten out of the bathtub, wrapped herself in her long blue terry robe, and was just about to make a snack of peanut butter and pickles and settle down with a TV movie when the doorbell rang. One thing was different, though. This time there were five long-stemmed red roses sitting in a vase on her coffee table.

Ken stood in the circle of porch light when she opened the door, and Faith gave a cry of delight and surprise when she saw what he held: the ribbons of a dozen multicolored balloons that bobbed and tugged with the breeze.

"Flowers seemed redundant," he explained with a grin, and it caught Faith by surprise, the swift wonder and bubbling of blinding joy that swept through her.

After what seemed like an eternity of separation he was
there on her doorstep, standing in the yellow glow of
her porch light, all that meant life and promise and per-
fection to Faith. He was no longer a shadowy figure
half-obscured by the haze of immortality, but real and
solid in plain brown slacks and an oxford shirt with the
cuffs folded up. His eyes were laughing and his brown
hair tousled, the fingers of one hand around the color-
ful ribbons of that absurd bouquet of balloons...and
everything that was within Faith seemed to come bursting and bubbling through. She flung herself into his
arms.

Ken gave a startled laugh as he stepped across the
threshold, his own arms coming around her and tightening in an embrace. His laughing lips touched her
neck; he smelled of something sweet and woodsy, like
life itself. And when he looked down at her the pleasure sparks in his eyes seemed to ignite little rivulets of
flame beneath Faith's skin, the glow of welcome in his
face warmed her just as intensely, just as solidly, as his
body had done when she was wrapped in his arms.

He moved one hand to close the door behind them,
and his eyes flickered over her, noticing first the flush
of her face and the bright welcome in her eyes, the
parted lips and the upward-tilted face, and he was
unable to disguise the quick dart of desire that answered her invitation. Then he registered her attire, the
fresh warm scent of soap and steam that emanated
from her skin, and his smile almost managed to be
apologetic. "It's late, I know," he said. "I just dropped
by to bring you these—" he transferred the balloon rib-

bons from his hand to hers "—and to tell you that we've been invited to South Bend for dinner on Monday to celebrate my sister's birthday." While he spoke his eyes were moving over her face with eagerness and a tautly restrained hunger, and with each word his voice grew softer, close to breathless toward the end, and Faith did not think he was much aware of what he was saying. "And to ask you—" his finger moved to stroke her cheek, his face seemed to be drawing closer "—if you missed me."

But barely were the words spoken before his lips were upon hers and Faith's helpless response was her answer. Her arms wound around his neck, her body curved into his. The balloons drifted from the anchor of her fingers and bounced against the ceiling. She opened herself to him without meaning to, without planning to, drawing him into her, wrapping herself around him. Caution was forgotten, all those desperate warnings from logic that she had examined and reexamined over the past week might never have existed at all. All the good and perfect reasons she should disappear from Ken's life forever evaporated into one simple truth, and that truth was that she loved him and she didn't think she could stop, not ever.

With careful wonder and mounting joy Ken accepted all she was offering him, reading from her body the words she had, until this point, been too afraid to say. His mouth possessed her with sweetness and promise that slowly grew to a dizzying demand, and his hands began to move restlessly over her body as passion built, weakening Faith and inflaming her. Each movement he made was a new catch in Faith's breath, a renewed jar to the rhythm of her pulse, which pushed heat and senselessness through her veins. His hands were hot and deliberately restrained against the back of her neck, beneath her hair, fingers stroking and caressing her earlobes, then firmer in their demand as they moved down her back, tracing and pressing the shape of her spine, the curve of her waist, moving to her buttocks and feeling the nakedness underneath the material, strong fingertips exploring her shape and pressing her into him. Faith could feel the hardening of his body and the pounding of his heart and the unsteady fan of his breath across her face as he placed slow and evocative kisses across her mouth and her cheeks and her neck. Her face turned to meet him, her lips catching his, her tongue brushing his, and through the white-hazed pleasure that whirled within her Faith knew this was getting out of control—soon now there would be no turning back....

It was Ken who pulled away, gently, reluctantly and barely by inches. His hands rested on her waist, his lips lingered on her cheek. And then he lifted his face, looking at her. His eyes were hazy and unfocused, the deep soft green of crushed velvet but with the light of a hundred candles flickering in their depths. His face was heated and Faith could see a sheen of dampness there, the tautness and alertness of every nerve fiber exposed to its sensitive roots. Faith knew what he was feeling because what she saw in his face was only a reflection of the aching within her own body.

"Faith," he whispered huskily. His hands moved upward to cup and tighten around handfuls of her hair. "I do want you." And the very slightest hint of a smile touched his lips as his eyes searched hers hesitantly, caressingly. "I guess that's another redundancy."

Yet beneath the urgency in his face there was a cautious question. He was offering her the opportunity to be very certain what she was doing this time. And with those simple words "I want you," with the caring, needing look, the truth of who they were and what they were about to do hit Faith with a shock; passion drained out of her and was replaced with the cold rushing stream of reality. She turned quickly and groped for the ribbons of the balloons that dangled at her cheek, managing a weak, fleeting smile. "I—I guess I'd better put these in water or something."

But before she even completed the turn, his hands fell upon her shoulders with gentle restraint. He turned her back to him. The gentle humor that she was so used to seeing in his face was gone now, his eyes were dark with confusion. He looked at her for a long time, probing her, and at last her eyes could no longer hold out against his relentless quest for an explanation; she dropped her lashes. And slowly he released her shoulders; she could sense the restrained confusion of hurt that filtered through his breath. He did not move, and neither did she. They stood inches apart, not touching. And at last Ken said, quietly, "Chelsy said she saw you at the service last night."

Faith nodded wordlessly, still unable to look at him.

For a moment Ken said nothing, then he moved past her, busying himself with tying the balloons to the top of a lamp shade. They bounced there with a carnival gaiety that contrasted sharply with the tensions vibrating within the room. "So," he said, with his back to her. His voice was flat. "What are you having trouble dealing with now? The idol, or the feet of clay?"

She cast a quick, bewildered glance his way, and he turned. His eyes were opaque. "You heard the story of my life last night," he said. He shrugged one shoulder lightly, and tried to smile. "I tell it so often that sometimes I forget how it must sound to someone hearing it for the first time. Does it bother you that I'm not as perfect as you thought I was? Or—" and his eyes clouded with the admission of what had, in fact, been his greatest fear all week "—was last night just your final try at fitting into a minister's life, and you found out you couldn't do it?"

The incredulity in her eyes slowly softened into wordless denial, and when she closed her eyes and tilted her head back with a long, slow sigh, the gentle affection that traced a smile across her lips was mixed with helplessness. He thought that she would stand in condemnation of his past. He thought that she could measure him and find him wanting. If only he knew...

She looked at him, and the anxiety that tightened the lines at the corners of his mouth pulled at her heart. "No, Ken," she said gently. "Neither of those things. I came last night because I wanted to... see what your life was like, the parts of it that I was afraid I wouldn't fit into, and..."

"And?" he prompted very softly when she stumbled. He seemed almost to be holding his breath. Was it possible he cared so much? How could it be that her decision, her acceptance or rejection of him and what he was, could mean so much to him? How could she deserve a man like this?

But the very least she owed him was honesty. Faith crossed one arm absently over her chest, rubbing the other briefly in a tight, nervous motion, but she would not drop her eyes. She let everything that was written there open itself up to him. "And," she said softly, with difficulty, "it made me cry."

She saw the lines of tension on his face cautiously relax, a thin light of hope began to burn through the clouds in his eyes. "I—I saw the whole man," she went on, and her voice was growing tight with the effort to tell a truth that was more painful than a lie could have been. "Everything that makes you the very special person you are and... it was so beautiful it made me cry."

"Darling." The word was a soft exclamation, and in two steps he was beside her. A forefinger crooked under her chin, lifting her face to him when she would have turned away. Beneath the happiness and the relief she saw in the eyes of the man she loved there was still confusion, and it translated into an amusement that coaxed her to smile. "Then what's the problem? A minute ago, what I felt from you when you were kissing me, and holding me... but then you looked at me, and you went stiff. Something is still bothering you, and I don't..." To Faith's very great discomfort, she felt a tingle of heat crawl upward to her face, and beneath his worried scrutiny it only grew worse.

"It's sex, isn't it?" Ken said, and amusement mixed

with the soft surprise in his voice. "Faith, look at me—it is, isn't it?"

But Faith would not look at him. He made it sound so simplistic, so easily dismissible, and it wasn't. It wasn't at all. "It's—complicated," she mumbled, averting her eyes, and could only hope that he would accept, and understand, what an understatement that was.

He dropped his finger from her chin and instead slipped his arm around her neck, so that the back of her head was cradled in his elbow and her cheek was cupped in his hand. He tilted his head until his face was in her direct line of vision and she could not look away. Such a beautiful face. Such a sweet, kind and patient face. How she loved every inch of it.

"Are the complications," he asked reasonably, "because I'm a minister and everyone knows that men of the cloth are completely immune to carnal urges—or are they because I'm a man and you're a woman and we're both experiencing some pretty strong carnal urges at this stage of our relationship?"

He wanted to make her smile, and Faith wished she could comply. She took a breath, and released it unsteadily. "A—little of both, I guess," she said, hoping he could not guess, praying he would not guess, how much deeper than that it went.

But something in her tone sobered Ken.

"Faith," he said quietly, "you know I would never hurt you, don't you?"

Faith looked into those gentle, absorbing eyes, and she could do nothing but nod.

Ken once again tried to coax her with a smile. "So

what is this? Do I have to give you my famous lecture on premarital sex?"

Faith pulled away, crossing her arms over her chest as she walked a few steps across the room. She did not know what to say, what to do. She only knew that one last time, before it was too late, she had to give him a chance. "Ken," she said tightly. She took a breath before turning. "I—I'm not exactly a virgin."

Ken's eyes twinkled tolerantly, though he managed to keep his face very sober. "Darling," he confessed, "neither am I."

And then he crossed the room to her, his face gentled with a mixture of compassion and concern. It must have been the distress on her face that convinced him at last to take her seriously, but he could have no idea what that distress reflected. Faith should have told him then; it would have been the perfect time, so easy, so natural. She should have told him, with the same confidence and lack of pretense that he had told his own story the night before; she should have gotten it over with, made a clean breast of it before things went any further and she lost her courage altogether...but already Faith knew that that was as close as she would ever come to telling Ken the truth. She simply couldn't tell him, couldn't bear to see the withdrawal and the condemnation in his eyes...couldn't face the hurt and disappointment there. She would never tell him. He would have to find out from someone else.

And when he did, it would destroy him.

Ken took her hands and guided her over to the sofa, pulling her down to sit beside him. He kept her hands covered with his, wrapped in his warmth, and he angled his body to look at her, so that their knees were touching. In his face was nothing but tenderness, his eyes were simple and sincere. His tone was quiet. "Faith," he asked, "how old are you?"

"Twenty-eight," she answered, and her lips barely moved. She was both miserable with her own cowardice and elated for the presence of this man whom she had no right to love, and the mixture of emotions were tearing her apart.

Ken nodded. "I'm thirty-two," he answered. "It would be foolish, don't you think, for either of us to imagine there had been no other lovers until now? Faith, I'm not jealous of your other boyfriends. I don't care what you did before you met me. I only care about you and me, together."

She wanted so badly to believe that. She wanted it so badly that for the moment she did believe it, and the hope and the desperation that flooded through her radiated in her eyes. She pulled her hands away and wrapped her arms about Ken, holding him tightly, pressing him to her, praying that it was possible never to let him go. And she couldn't help it, she whispered into his neck, "I love you!"

Ken's arms, which had begun automatically to encircle her, stopped midway to her shoulders. "What?" he breathed. He took her arms, he pushed her away from him. He searched her face with hope and thinly disguised anxiety jumping and darting in his eyes. "What did you say?"

A combination of crazy emotions were twisting and

cavorting inside Faith. The words were spoken and could not be taken back, and she was glad. For the first time in her life she had done the right thing, and she was sure of it. It was over and she felt light, free, like the bouncing colored balloons that would take right off into heaven if they weren't anchored down. The wonder of it, combined with that vulnerable expression of incredulity on Ken's face, was too much to be contained, and she laughed out loud. "I said I love you!" she cried, and then she was in his arms again.

They held each other, simply held each other, tightly, deeply, never wanting to let go. His heartbeat became synchronized with hers, his breath took on the rhythm of hers. Faith could not tell where her body began and his ended, so close were they; so much a part of each other, mind and body and soul, did they become in the endless moment of silent embrace that there did not seem to be a time when they had ever been separate, nor would they be again.

Then Ken lifted his face a little and looked down at her. The glow in his eyes was so deep, so absorbing and all-encompassing that it took her breath away—it blinded her to everything but the infinity that lay within his eyes. "Faith," he whispered, "you know that I love you, don't you? You know that I really am going to marry you?"

She looked up at him, helpless with the miracle she saw in his face. She didn't understand it, the wonder of it was too much, but somehow it was true, it was really happening to her. And all she could do was say, hardly above a whisper, "How...can you love me?"

His eyes closed slowly; helplessness softened the lines of his face. The curve of his lips was adoring as he opened his eyes again, lifting one finger to trace the shape of her face from temple to jaw. "Don't you know," he said simply, "what happened to me when you tumbled off that ladder and into my arms that first day? I looked into your eyes and I saw right into your soul. I saw the other half of me there, Faith, all the strength and goodness and purity I wished I had." And when she took a sharp breath, he laid his finger lightly across her lips to still her. "It was like—" for the first time he struggled briefly with the words "—a jolt, a slap...something I can't explain and I couldn't forget. I knew I had to know you, I couldn't let you out of my life."

And he smiled a little. "I told you I'm impulsive, but you've got to believe me, I've never behaved that way with a woman in my life. I pursued you even when you didn't want me. I did crazy things to get your attention. And I would have kept on pursuing you, kept on doing crazier and crazier things until I found out for sure what I did, eventually, learn—that you really were as perfect as I thought in that first moment." He lowered his eyes briefly, and when he looked at her again his eyes were so clear, so earnest, that it broke her heart.

"It was a strange thing, Faith," he said soberly. "Do you remember I told you about the Unseen Hand? This is what I was talking about. Sometimes, very rarely, life just hits you with these brief, powerful glimpses of insight—like a door opening on the way you were surely meant to go. You can't explain it, but there's a feeling that's just as clear and just as strong as anything you've ever known. It's only happened to me twice," he told her simply. "The first time I got that feeling was when I answered the call to the ministry. The second time was when I looked into your eyes."

And then something began to coil within Faith, an awful feeling of premonition, the stirring of the forces that she had so willfully tried to put to death, those hissing and whispering little voices that told her this was wrong, it was evil to deceive him, it could only lead to disaster. How could she look into those clear, soul-encompassing eyes and lie?

"Ken," she whispered weakly, her eyes pleading with him to understand, to see within her what she could not put into words, to save himself before she destroyed him. "I'm...not what you think I am. I'm not good, I—"

"You are," he told her quietly, "perfect for me. You are tender, sweet and caring. You have a compassion for people and an understanding of human nature that goes beyond anything I've ever seen before. You can reach people." And he smiled. "Just look what you've done with Chelsy in less than a week."

Faith lowered her eyes uncomfortably. If only it were true. If only all those things he said about her were true, and if only they were enough. "I didn't do anything with Chelsy," she protested.

Gently, Ken lifted her face into his smiling eyes. "Darling," he said, "you gave her hope. If you had taken even one good look at her last night, you would know that."

Faith looked at him, and she was convinced that as long as she could look into his eyes and see herself reflected there, see all the goodness and the wonder that he thought existed within her, perhaps she could truly be that person. As long as she could keep her eyes on Ken, she could be nothing less than perfect.

He leaned forward and buried his lips briefly in her hair. "Do you know something else?" he murmured huskily. "Right now I want to make love to you more than anything else in the world." And he smiled. "So much for my immunity against the frailties of the flesh. But—" he lifted his hand to smooth her hair behind her ear, his expression sobering "—when I do it will be forever, a lifetime commitment. It doesn't matter if it's tonight, or a week from tonight, or on our wedding night—whenever you're ready to make that same kind of commitment to me," he told her simply, "we'll go to bed together. And I can wait as long as it takes."

Faith looked at him, and the simple sincerity in his eyes freed her at last to the final flowering of hope. She wanted so badly to believe. And perhaps if she believed hard enough, if she wanted it badly enough, the miracle would be hers.

I'll be a good wife to you, Ken, she determined quietly. *I'll be all that you expect me to be and all that you see in me and more. Nothing that is within my power to prevent will ever hurt you. No one will ever know the secrets that could destroy you, and it has nothing to do with us. I'm different now. The past is behind me, and with you in my future there is nothing I can't do. I'll love you, Ken, more than anyone else could ever love you, and I'll bring the best to you.*

And then her lips tightened with a small, shy, half-teasing smile, and she suggested, "What if we're not compatible—in bed?"

His eyes sparked. Deliberately he traced his finger around her lips, downward to her chin, and resting at last on her throat, testing the quick pulse there. "Are you really worried about that?" he challenged softly. And then he smiled, folded his hand to nuzzle the line of her jaw. "If we're not compatible," he decided, "we'll learn how to be. There are books written on the subject, you know. There's a solution for every problem, Faith," he teased gently, and his eyes waited for the answer to the question he had been asking since the very first moment they met.

Faith wanted to give it to him. Had another second passed uninterrupted she would have. And it was as though her silent decision, the false certainty that was about to prompt her into a step from which there would be no turning back summoned forces wiser and more powerful than she. It was the ringing of the telephone that saved her, and Ken, from what she was about to say.

Because Faith's telephone rarely ever rang at night, it startled her. Ken's patient smile gave her permission to answer it, and he moved away as she murmured, "It's probably just a wrong number."

But it wasn't a wrong number. The voice on the

other end said, "Miss Hilliard? This is Officer Brad-cock with the Little Creek Police. There's been an incident at your shop, and I think you'd better come down here."

Chapter Eleven

Too good to be true, too good to be true... that was the phrase that echoed in Faith's head over and over again during that next nightmarish hour, and would recur to haunt her constantly in the coming days. She had stepped in where she did not belong, she had upset the delicate balance of things by trying to move into Ken's life, and this was the first warning movement of the hand of Fate, telling her it would never work.

Only moments ago they had been sitting in Faith's warm, lamplit house, holding each other, loving each other, about to make promises to each other that would last a lifetime. Now they were standing in the chill night air on the street in front of her shop, broken glass littering the sidewalk, red-and-blue lights making crazy arcs around them. The crackle of low-band radios cluttered up the still spring evening and a crowd was gathering. At the edge of that crowd two police cars—the entire sum of Little Creek's law enforcement agency—were parked at angles, and against one of them stood Tony, his hands cuffed behind his back, his knees sagging, his head dropping weakly. There was an angry red bruise rising on his cheek and blood trickled from his mouth.

Immediately Ken started toward him, but a uniformed officer caught his arm. "I wouldn't try to talk to him, Reverend," the officer said curtly. "He's so strung out he wouldn't know you."

Ken turned on the man, the muscles in his cheek tightening, his eyes narrowed to blazing slits in the eerie flash of light. Anger radiated from him in short, snapping waves and seemed to mingle with and draw from the incredibly charged atmosphere that surrounded them, all of it spinning out of control. "That boy has been beaten!" Ken accused.

The officer returned his gaze coldly. "You should see what he did to one of my men," he returned, very low. "It took three of us to pull him off. The officer who went through that window—" he jerked his head shortly to the crumbled glass and gaping hole that had once been the showcase of Faith's shop; a trampled basket of silk daisies tipped drunkenly through the hole and Faith remembered incoherently that Chelsy had put that arrangement, one of her best, in the window only today "—he'll be lucky if he makes it through the night, and if he doesn't—" the officer's face darkened, his voice clipped "—your boy's in a lot of trouble. A hell of a lot."

Faith saw Ken's hands clench at his sides, she saw the stern, hard lines of his profile as he turned back to look at Tony, and her stomach was hollow, her thoughts and her emotions as shattered as the glass that crunched under her feet. From far away the officer's voice filtered down to her, "I'm sorry about all the damage, Miss Hilliard. A lot of it was done before we got here. Apparently all he was after was the cash box, but when these kids get dusted there's no telling what they'll do."

Faith looked at him numbly. "Dusted?" she repeated hesitantly.

"Angel dust." The short, harsh voice was Ken's. He was still looking at Tony. "PCP."

Angel dust, Faith repeated dully to herself, absently. What an odd phrase for something so ugly, so violent...but appropriate somehow. Like a dirty joke. Faith said out loud, "What happened?" But she really didn't want to know. It really didn't matter. The words, the details, were all irrelevant, because the graphic evidence of tragedy was littered all over the sidewalk and flashing in red-and-blue lights across Ken's granite-white face....

"We got the call at nine-eleven," the officer replied, checking his notebook. "An anonymous tip. We apprehended the young man at nine-seventeen inside the shop with one hundred fifty dollars in his pocket that had apparently come from your cash box. We'll need a complete statement from you about that, Miss Hilliard." He looked at her, not bothering to disguise the accusation in his voice. "You shouldn't leave cash in your shop over the weekend."

Faith nodded dully. She knew that. She should have known that, but it was such a small town, and so quiet. Saturday was her biggest day for cash receipts and the banks weren't open. She had never worried about it before.

"He was already starting to smash things around when we got here," the officer went on, and then he looked at her meaningfully. "But he entered with a key. He still had it on him. Who else has a key to your shop, Miss Hilliard?"

Chelsy.

Faith's eyes met Ken's, and just when she thought the nightmare could not get any darker, it did. Chelsy, whom she had trusted with her business, her van, her key... Chelsy, for whom she had had such high hopes... Chelsy, who had only been another bad judgment.

"We've got to know who else had a key, Miss Hilliard," the officer insisted somewhat roughly.

Ken turned and walked away from her.

"My—my assistant," Faith said hoarsely. And there was no point in fighting it any longer. An incredible weariness came over her as she said, "Her name is Chelsy Warren. She's from the Crossroads, too." And then suddenly she looked at the officer. "What," she managed, "what will happen if I don't press charges?"

The officer didn't even look up from the notations he was making on his pad. "Won't make any difference, Miss Hilliard. That kid already has half a dozen felony charges on him, including three counts of assaulting a police officer... maybe murder."

How could this happen, Faith thought in blank-eyed despair, looking around at the destruction that littered the sidewalk, the grim-faced uniforms that moved in and out of the circles of red-and-blue light like specters from some screenwriter's version of hell. How could it have happened here, in this quiet place, the eruption of all the ugliness and violence Faith had fled from in Chicago over two years ago? And a small, sinister voice whispered, *Maybe you bring it with you....*

Ken had walked over to Tony. The officer who guarded the young man looked at Ken warily, but Ken reached out to touch Tony's shoulder lightly. The boy's head jerked upright. "Well, my friend," Ken said quietly, "you've gone and done it this time, haven't you?" The wild-eyed incoherency in Tony's face frightened Faith. And Ken continued to speak softly. "I don't know what I can do for you this time, but I'm going to try. But I need your help. You've got to..."

Tony threw his head back and spat deliberately in Ken's face.

Faith took an involuntary step in his direction, pulled as though someone had grabbed the muscles of her heart with a single determined tug that threatened to rip the organ from her body. But just then Tony erupted into a fit of wild thrashing and a gush of violent, screaming profanity that sent another officer to the aid of the first and stripped Faith of reason or capacity for movement. Ken stood there like a statue until Tony was shoved into the police car and it sped away, lights flashing in ever-diminishing circles, across the quiet streets of an innocent spring night. Then he lifted his hand slowly to wipe the spittle from his chin, and he turned and walked away.

"Miss Hilliard." A touch on her arm, the sound of the voice, filtered down to Faith through the din of confusion and hurt that knew only one purpose—to go to Ken, to be with him, to comfort him if she could. Faith glanced back distractedly. The officer said, "Would it be too much trouble for you to come down to the station and give a statement tonight?"

"No..." Faith replied absently, and hardly heard her own words. She was moving toward Ken. "I'll be there... in a minute..."

Ken was leaning against the wall of her building, hands stuffed into his pockets, eyes staring grimly straight ahead. His desolation emanated toward Faith in waves, like the undulating lights from the one remaining patrol car that turned his face first to chalk-white then to violent red. Faith half-lifted her hand to touch him, but let it fall away helplessly. His face was as hard as stone.

And then as she stood there, wanting to say something, to do something, to ease his pain, he whispered tightly, through clenched teeth, "Damn." It was a harsh syllable, low and vicious and releasing within it all the helplessness, all the fury and the senseless waste that this night symbolized. He closed his eyes slowly; he leaned his head back against the wall. Faith could see the pain that was tearing at his face, and it was her own. The tightening of his lips could have been an effort to smile, or to hold back tears, but it was a fleeting thing, crossing like a phantom through the night and leaving only bleakness. "We lost this one," he said simply, and then, after a moment, he groped for her hand.

Faith's fingers closed about his and tightened, and they clung to each other in that moment of desolation and defeat, shared pain and equal loss. But a single handclasp seemed very frail protection against the forces of destruction that Faith could sense building around them.

THE EXPERIENCE HOVERED over Faith like a lingering illness, entwined as it was with the residue of doubt and self-blame, threatening to leave her permanently shaken. But Ken was more resilient. "It happens," he told her briefly as he drove her home from the shop Monday afternoon, where he had finally persuaded her to leave the most difficult repair jobs to the professionals, who would be arriving first thing tomorrow morning. "You never get used to it, it never stops hurting, but—it happens. There are still ten more kids out at the Crossroads I have a chance with, and hundreds more I haven't even reached yet, and you have to just put the past behind you. Cut your losses and move on."

But for Faith the past was a persistent shadow, lurking in corners and leaping out in unexpected places, dogging her every footstep and reminding her that there is no place to hide when all you're running from is yourself. Tony chouldn't change; Chelsy couldn't change. Was Faith really all that different?

She did not understand why, with all the other businesses in town, most of them far more profitable than her obscure little shop, they had chosen to risk everything for a mere one hundred fifty dollars and the sound of breaking glass.

"Besides the fact that Chelsy had a key and knew how much money you had." Ken answered, and shrugged. "Sometimes people will strike out at the ones closest to them for nothing more than the satisfaction of it. Biting the hand that feeds you is a very effective form of self-punishment."

Faith suppressed a shudder. She knew all about self-punishment.

Tony had positively identified Chelsy as his coconspirator and punctuated his story with many violent threats upon the girl's life if he ever caught up with her. They had apparently planned the escapade together, and Chelsy had gone so far as to give him the key before deserting him. Chelsy had disappeared from the Crossroads, and if anyone knew anything about her whereabouts, no one was talking. Obviously one or more of the kids had gotten wind of the plan beforehand, thus the anonymous phone call to the police, but whoever it was apparently felt he had done his civic duty and was offering no further help.

Faith thought about the girl, so innocent despite her bravado, and she felt sick inside. Ken saw the same goodness and innocence in Faith that he had seen inside Chelsy, but did people ever really change? Was the line between good and bad really so easy to distinguish? Faith had believed in Chelsy, and the consequences had been tragic. Ken believed in Faith, but wasn't this a sign of what could happen when trust was misplaced? Couldn't this be a warning that the same fate awaited Faith somewhere yet down the road? But those were the rumblings and murmurings of her conscience that Faith simply could not afford to listen to right now.

Ken gently and determinedly tried to erase her guilt, apologizing to her for the trouble he felt responsible for bringing to her. Sharing the responsibility and the sorrow was an easing of the burden, for Faith knew Ken was suffering, and worrying about Chelsy, at least as much as she was. They sought and accepted each other's support, and that part of it was a discovery that was almost worth the tragedy it had taken to reach it. She could help Ken. She could look at him and see the easing of the pain in his eyes, and know that he needed her. The sharing of a time of trouble was even sweeter than the sharing of love, and through it strength grew. They depended on each other. Maybe, from the midst of a disaster, they could wrest a miracle. But beneath it all, the uncertain shadows of guilt and deception shifted and stirred, and Faith doubted it.

She should have known that all the while that Unseen Hand was moving to arrange her destiny. She should have felt the shifting and the cracking of the ground beneath her feet that was even now preparing to open up and swallow whole the careful illusion of a future she had built. She should have known better, but she didn't.

FROM THE BEGINNING, Faith was uneasy about the dinner arrangements in South Bend, the meeting of Ken's sister, the intrusion of her presence on what should have been strictly a family celebration. The reasons for that were obvious, and simply too childish to share with Ken. By introducing Faith to his sister on such a special occasion, Ken was all but announcing to his family that this was a woman of whom they could expect to see a lot in the future. It made Faith uneasy to be scrutinized in that way. But she would not have disappointed Ken by canceling. He had had far too many disappointments lately, and this evening of resuming a normal life would be good for him—possibly for both of them.

It was womanly vanity, and girlish nervousness, that made Faith want to look her very best that evening. Ken had told her that reservations had been made in one of the finer restaurants, and for the occasion, Faith reached into the back of her closet for a remnant of her former life.

Even at the height of her success, Faith had not been a flashy dresser. Discretion, femininity and allure—that was the image that had made Copper Adams famous. The blouse she chose was a pale pink crepe, which, in former days, she had worn rarely because it clashed with her hair in most lights. Now, however, the rosy color only highlighted traces of strawberry in her hair and added much-needed radiance to her cheeks. The blouse, with its puffed sleeves and high ruffles, was demure yet sophisticated, and when coupled with a slim black floor-length skirt of taffeta moiré, gave her an elegant and understated appearance.

Stress and sleepless nights had had their usual effect on Faith. Her face was fragile and white, her eyes dark-circled, her hair limp. She applied more makeup than usual, and she could not help thinking about the last time she had sat in front of this makeup box, with Chelsy an avid and wondering student. She applied a rosy lip gloss, pulled her hair into an upsweep, and had a few minutes before Ken rang the bell to scrutinize her appearance. She looked good. She hadn't gotten this dressed up since she had left Chicago, and it was a funny feeling to look into the mirror and see a reflection of her former self stare back at her. It made a shiver crawl up her spine, but the premonitory sense of foreboding evaporated like nothing more than the mist it was the minute she opened the door and saw the light of surprise and pleasured appreciation fill Ken's eyes. "You are," he said softly, "more beautiful than I ever thought anyone could be."

The glow that kindled within Faith lasted all the way to South Bend, and nothing else mattered except that when Ken looked at her he saw beauty.

Faith's uneasiness returned the moment Ken introduced her to his sister. It was just a flash of something in the other woman's eyes—a startled curiosity, a hint of disapproval—and it was gone so quickly that Faith could almost convince herself she had imagined it. For almost immediately the woman was clasping both her hands, beaming warmly, and telling Faith how delighted she was to meet her after all Ken had told them about her. The welcome was genuine, the pleasure unfeigned. Faith forced her qualms to subside.

Ken's sister was as open and easy to know as Ken himself, and her husband was a down-to-earth friendly man who obviously adored his wife. Both regarded Faith with great warmth, as if they had been waiting all their lives to meet the unique woman in the life of someone special to them, and before Faith knew it, she was allowing herself to relax in this simple communal atmosphere. She could be a part of this life, she realized finally, completely. She could belong to these people and they to her. She could be happy sharing Ken's life, the good and the bad, the troubles and the joys... and she wanted it more than anything in the world.

They laughed and they talked, and Faith was included among them as though she had always been part of the family. Ken's sister Amelia teased him by telling cute anecdotes of his childhood and Ken got even with her by pretending to spot imaginary gray hairs and wrinkles and missing no opportunity to remind everyone that the reason for this celebration was the occasion of her thirtieth birthday. They were a wonderful pair, unabashed in their playful affection for each other, concerned with each other's lives, and Faith found herself anxious to meet their parents. She knew she was going to love this family as she did her own.

And then, with absolutely no warning at all, the glorious cloud of euphoric optimism that had surrounded Faith all evening dispersed abruptly into harsh and unforgiving reality.

It was a simple thing, hardly a beat lost in the celebratory tempo that had carried them through dinner, nothing to signal alarm or cause concern to anyone... except Faith. It was simply that as coffee was served, Amelia looked across the table at Faith, and the pleasant camaraderie in her eyes was tempered this time with a measure of puzzlement. It was a gaze Amelia had obviously not expected Faith to catch, because when their eyes met, Amelia gave an embarrassed little laugh. "I'm sorry," she said. "You must think I'm incredibly rude, the way I've been staring at you all night."

Faith had not noticed Amelia's staring. A little shiver started to run up her spine.

Amelia's husband laughed. "Oh-oh! Next thing you know she'll be pestering me about why I never buy her outfits as pretty as yours. She's probably been sitting here trying to memorize the design."

Amelia gave her husband a playful slap on the arm, and Faith tried to keep her smile from fading. She should have made some joke, then, some offhand remark designed to change the subject, but she couldn't think of one. Her mind was a blank, and she knew what was going to happen next. It was as though she had been waiting for this all evening...longer than that.

"No," Amelia retorted, "I'm just trying to figure out how Kenny ever snagged a woman as beautiful as Faith! Who would have thought it?"

Ken grinned and slipped an arm around Faith's shoulders, giving her a brief squeeze. "Sheer charm, little sister," he assured her. "You ought to try it sometime."

For a moment, Faith almost thought the opportunity would pass. The dread eased from her stomach, she started to relax. She should have known better.

Amelia looked back at Faith, curiosity overcoming her playfulness. "Actually," she said, rather seriously, "the moment I first saw you, I had the feeling we'd met before. I've been sitting here all evening trying to

figure out where, and I finally decided what it was."
Slowly, Faith felt the cold blanket of certainty descend
on her.

Amelia turned from her brother to her husband with
the air of one harboring a delightful secret. "Of course
neither of you two morons would notice, but Faith
looks just like someone famous—we've seen her picture a thousand times, on TV, or in magazines—" and
her brow clouded a little, overshadowing her air of vic-
tory "—only I can't think just who. It'll come to me in
a minute," she insisted, as both her husband and Ken
began to laugh, teasing her ruthlessly about the onset
of senility.

No one noticed the color that drained from Faith's
cheeks, nor that she did not join in the joking speculation about what famous person Amelia had in mind. It
was such a small thing, little more than two minutes'
conversation in an evening filled with bright and bubbly talk, hardly worth remembering or remarking upon
once the initial entertainment value was gone. And no
one noticed that within those two brief minutes of joking and lighthearted teasing Faith's world had come to
a very quiet and very predictable end.

Amelia knew. It might not be clear to her now, but
tomorrow, or later on tonight...a week, or a month
from now... She would be sorting out a stack of old
magazines, and Faith's picture would leap off the
cover. She would wake her husband in the middle of
the night, the puzzle solved. She would start searching
out old copies of *Time* and *Newsweek*, and the DeFrancis story would be there waiting. How long had Faith

really thought she could get away with this? Who was she trying to kid? It was only a matter of time....

And if not Amelia, someone else. As soon as she and Ken started making their relationship more public, the curiosity of his parishioners would be aroused. It was a small town, but not completely isolated. The townspeople were not stupid. It wouldn't take them long. Not long at all.

They lingered over coffee, laughing and talking and acting for all the world as though this were the happiest night of their lives. But Faith was removed for it, separated by the cloudy veil of the past from what she wanted and could not have. Faith could only watch, and accept, and resign herself to the fact that she could not hide any longer. And amid all the warmth and gaiety that surrounded her, Faith felt the slow cold draining of everything that was beautiful and good and promising leave her body and pool lifelessly at her feet. She saw the glimmering veil of illusion dry and crinkle and wisp into ashes, leaving nothing between her vision and the hard evidence of reality that had always been there, that she had refused to see.

The fantasy was over, and it was time to face the truth.

Somehow Faith survived the rest of the evening, though she remembered little about it. A dull, numbing shock had gripped her, muting the laughter, dimming the lights, blurring the faces. She was not even aware of the feel or the movements of her own body—lips that stretched to smile, fingers that lifted a coffee cup, vocal cords that formed words. She was detached from it all, a person apart, looking down from afar and watching the carefully built illusion that was the life of Faith Hilliard come to a very predictable end, feeling no surprise, no sorrow. Feeling nothing.

But under that blanket of shock her mind was working very coolly, very precisely. She wondered what these kind, laughing people, so securely wrapped up in their bright little middle-class world, would say if they knew they were having dinner with a mobster's mistress. If ever she had harbored some dim hope that Ken, when he did find out, would overlook her past sins, it was gone now. Sitting there with his slightly plump sister and her slightly bald husband, listening to them talk about children and schools, and church work and mission funds, Faith saw all too clearly how different their world was from hers. She had been a fool to think she could ever fit in.

Ken turned the radio on during the long drive home. He might have tried to make conversation, but if he did, Faith did not remember. She did remember the way his hand felt, holding hers. Soft. It made her own hand feel rough and clawlike to Faith's perception, and very cold.

The only wonder to her was how easily she had almost convinced herself this could work. How effectively Ken had woven his spell around her and made her believe in the possibility of things only hoped for... but her eyes were opened now to the harsh truth. Ken lived in a world where unicorns flew over rainbows and myths were the substance of life, and where miracles could happen if only you believed strongly enough. In the real world, the world in which Faith lived, faces were bought and sold like cheap perfume, courtly, debonair men ran drugs and defrauded the government, and the best of relationships lasted only until the cameras stopped clicking. In the real world there were no fairy-tale endings. Seventeen-year-old boys fried their brains on PCP and ended up in the county jail, waiting to be charged with murder. Sixteen-year-old girls turned tricks on the street for ten dollars a shot, and nothing was pretty, nothing was perfect, nothing was safe. Nowhere did the two worlds intersect. Faith should have known that. She really should have.

Ken saw her inside to her living room. She did not notice the little lines of concern on his face, or the cloudiness in his eyes. When he touched her she pulled away, and it was a natural reflex action. He didn't belong to her anymore. He never really had.

Faith went over to where Lance was stretched out on the sofa. She bent to stroke him and he hissed at her. Faith smiled, very faintly.

Ken said quietly behind her, "All right, Faith, what's wrong?"

Faith stiffened, and whatever hope she had had for shielding herself from this confrontation behind the walls of numbness slipped away, slowly, inevitably. There was only Faith—who she was and what she was, past and present—stripped before him, and she had to face it. She had to face him.

Ken said, "Was it something that happened at dinner? I've been racking my brains, trying to remember if anyone said anything to offend you—I thought you were having a good time." His brow creased faintly with puzzlement. "Amelia really liked you, Faith, not that it was any kind of test, but I knew you were nervous about meeting her."

But Faith was hardly listening. She had walked over to the closet, very calmly, and reached up to the top shelf. She took down a stack of magazines—her favorite cover was on top—and a small scrapbook filled with press clippings. Perhaps the very fact that she had kept them told her how much she had really wanted to escape from the past...not very much at all.

She walked over to Ken and presented the magazine first. "Have you ever heard of a model called Copper Adams?"

She watched as Ken went through the predictable motions—staring at the magazine cover, staring at her. Watching astonishment widen his eyes. Watching him look back to the magazine cover. Hearing his voice, weak with confusion and other emotions not yet defined, murmur, "Why...it's you. It really is."

And then, the confusion in his eyes turned slowly to delight. "You must think I'm really stupid, but I don't keep up much with things like this. Why didn't you tell me, Faith? Imagine that! A cover girl!"

With absolutely no emotion at all, Faith squelched the wonder and pleasure in his eyes by opening the scrapbook. Her eyes were as remote as a mountain lake. "You may not keep up with cover girls," she said clearly, coldly, "but I don't think you could have missed the DeFrancis story. Maybe this will jog your memory." She shoved the book toward him.

It should have. hurt her, watching the color drain from his face, the warmth go out of his eyes. It should have torn her apart inside to see the way his knuckles whitened on the edges of the scrapbook and the way his face tightened until it resembled nothing more than a sculpted mask. She should have been aching for his pain, for his disappointment and his disillusionment, but in fact all she could feel was her own pain.

And the pain made her vicious. "What's the matter, Ken?" she said shortly. "Didn't I tell you I wasn't a virgin? That's right, I slept with DeFrancis—him and others like him. A lot of others," she exaggerated, for some wild and inexplicable reason wanting to twist the knife, to wound as she was wounded, to make him hate her as much as she hated herself. "And you know what else? I liked it! I liked the glamour and the power and the money, I liked being one of the most sought-after bedroom decorations in the country, and it didn't matter to me if my lovers were Congressmen or pimps, as long as they knew how to treat a lady! I liked Greg DeFrancis—we were good friends and we had some good times, and it never mattered to me what he did for a living—maybe I even liked that. Maybe I liked being known as the girlfriend of one of the most notorious criminals of the decade. Maybe the only thing I ever minded was getting caught!"

She had to stop on a choked breath, waiting for his reaction, stunned and infuriated when she got none. She had embellished the relationship between herself and DeFrancis, reinforcing the lies the gossip rags had told, but she felt no qualm for the exaggeration. Perversely, she wanted him to believe the worst. She wanted to hurt him.

Ken just stood there, looking at the scrapbook, calm and unruffled, and she didn't understand it. His silence only made her own pain and frustration harder to bear.

She was tired, tired of lies and pretenses and hoping for miracles, tired of believing in possibilities that didn't exist, tired of reaching for what she could never have. And she was angry. She was angry because it wasn't fair. She could not change the past, and he had no right to make her want to. She was angry because after all this time she had learned to live with it and deal with it and suddenly he came along making her ashamed, and guilty...angry because he stood there, not looking at her, not saying anything, making her do this to him...and suddenly it all burst within her and she cried, "Damn it, Ken, didn't you ever wonder about me? You say you love me, but you didn't even know me, you didn't even try, you didn't even care. Didn't it ever occur to you to wonder where I came from, what I did, *who I was?*"

He lifted his eyes to her but said nothing. He looked as though he could stand there forever saying nothing. "Maybe you thought it didn't matter," she accused him, breathing hard. "Maybe in your clean little fantasy world things like the past and a reputation can be overlooked...confess and be forgiven, right? Well, let me tell you something, Reverend, in real life things don't work that way. In real life, it does matter."

She whirled abruptly and strode to the closet, jerking open the door. She pushed aside cloth coats, Windbreakers and parkas and jerked out a long garment in a paper covering. Viciously she ripped off the paper to expose a full-length sable coat. "This matters," she spat, and she flung the garment at him. It landed in the middle of the floor between them, overturning the vase of roses on the coffee table along its way. "A gift from DeFrancis—a payoff, a bribe, who knows? But I kept it. Maybe I don't look like the same woman he gave it to, maybe I don't act like her, but I kept the damn coat! Because it matters!"

She looked at him, chest heaving, eyes narrowed, small hands bunched into the taffeta material against her thighs. A dangerous red stain crept across the whiteness of her cheekbones. "It never occurred to you to wonder," she taunted, "how I just happened to walk into town with enough money to set up my own shop and buy this house, an independent business-woman at age twenty-five? Thirty-five thousand dollars, Reverend," she spat at him, "all in cash!" And then she had to stop, drawing in burning, furious gulps of breath, and all she saw in his face was immobility, all she saw in his eyes was apathy.

And something within her wanted to twist the knife, to make him hurt as she was hurting, and she went on hatefully, spitefully. "Don't you think you should have done some investigating of your prospective bride? Wouldn't that have saved you a lot of embarrassment in the end? No woman makes that kind of money honestly, Ken," she said viciously, "and there were an awful lot of dirty compromises along the way. An awful lot. What do you think your congregation is going to

say about that?'' she flung at him. ''What will they
think when they find out their minister is keeping company with a glamour girl and the mistress of a mobster?
That might cause a bit of a credibility gap between you
and the people you're supposed to guide, mightn't it?''

She turned to him, face white, eyes glittering, hands
bunched into impotent fists at her sides. ''Well?'' she
demanded. Her voice was hoarse, and she thought she
might scream if he didn't say something...anything.
''Mightn't it?''

But Ken was not looking at her. He was looking at
the pool of sable on the floor, the spilled roses scattered
like tears across the coffee table, the steady, rhythmic
drip and click of water plopping onto the carpet. The
silence was empty, still, absorbing even the echo of her
last words. And it went on forever.

Then, at last, Ken looked up. His face was pale, his
expression blank. In his eyes there was no light at all,
but far beyond their murky depths something stirred,
like the final weak quivers of a wounded animal. He
looked at her for a very long time, and that emptiness,
that dead hopelessness seemed to pull at Faith's soul,
drawing it from her in a long, slow, exquisitely painful
gush, swallowing it up into the blank void that was his
eyes.

''So what are you waiting for me to do?'' Ken said
finally, very quietly. ''Cast the first stone?''

And that was it. That was all she could take. The
crumpling and twisting of horror and agonizing loss began deep down in the pit of Faith's stomach and spread
slowly upward. She stiffened herself against it, and she

couldn't even draw a breath; her eyes blazed with the effort of holding it inside, and they could not focus on him.

She whispered, with an effort that was barely audible, "Get out of here, Ken. Leave me alone."

Needle-sharp seconds that stabbed at her chest and burned in her eyelids ticked off to the dripping of spilled water and the sound of his quiet breathing—so silent, so empty, Faith almost imagined she could hear the slow rending sound of the breaking of his heart. And all the while it was building in her, the need to cry, to scream, to strike out blindly in wild retaliation or to sob out loud for all she had lost and could never regain....

She did not know how much longer she could fight it back, and she did not want Ken to see her like that. She did not want to cause him more pain, and most of all she did not want to see that blankness that was in his eyes now turn to pity and finally into hatred, but she did not know how much longer she could hold on.

Then, at last, at last, Ken moved. He bent to pick up the sable and folded it carefully across the sofa. Then he turned and walked out the door. There was nothing else he could do.

It was over.

Chapter Twelve

Faith almost did not go into the shop the next morning. The only thing that finally persuaded her was the fact that the glaziers were due to replace her picture window and the locksmith was expected to arrive with her new locks, and they wouldn't know what to do if they got there and no one was present to greet them. Responsibility, Faith reflected with a faint, fleeting smile, did crazy things to people.

She had not slept at all the night before, nor even gone to bed. She had cried until she made herself sick, releasing a dam of pent-up emotions of such depth and proportion that she had never before imagined it was possible for a human being to experience them and still survive. Maybe she had died a little during the night. Maybe all that was vital and important to her had started to die the moment she looked into Ken's eyes and saw nothing but emptiness there.

And empty was what she felt that morning. Purged and cleansed and exhausted, but empty. Every nerve fiber had been wrung to its fullest extension of pain, every emotional cord stripped. There simply wasn't anything left to hurt.

The shop did not look as bad as it had before Faith had been in on Sunday and Monday with broom and masking tape; in fact, the actual damage had never been as bad as she had suspected. The cooling unit had been preserved, so what live flowers she had ordered before the weekend were still intact, and Tony had not made it back to the greenhouse or the workroom.

Most of the artificial arrangements had been swept off the shelves and trampled by many careless feet; the shelves themselves, constructed of lightweight painted tin, were dented and chipped, some of them even twisted beyond repair. Wrought-iron skeletons were all that remained of two small glass display counters. A large plywood square had replaced her window, and the light inside was dusty, gray, barren. The little shop, once a bright spot of color and fragrance, a new beginning of a new life, had been raped of its innocence. It looked desolate, empty and devoid of hope.

Faith bent to pick up a crumpled wicker flower basket that had tumbled to a corner. Then she looked at it for a minute and let it slip from her fingers back to the floor. "What's the point?" she said softly, tiredly. She straightened up and looked around. The window would be replaced today, but the shelves wouldn't be in until later in the week. She could open up tomorrow if she wanted to, but what really was the point? What was left for her here?

Nothing but memories and disillusionment, the constant reminder of what she had reached for and lost ... and the haunting fear that around every corner, in any crowd, she could look up suddenly and see a face filled with pain and disappointment, a constant reminder of the life she had almost destroyed. Every time the phone rang, each time the bell clanged with the arrival of a new customer, every time a figure passed her shop and paused to look in, her heart would leap to her throat, hope would flare and then die, because there was no way to undo the past. It was over, and the miracle she had been waiting for would never come again. . . . Faith couldn't live like that.

If she sold her inventory and her house it would give her enough for a new start. A new town, a new life, some place far away where shadows couldn't find her and memories wouldn't haunt her.

Faith had left the door open, and at the scuffle of movement she turned, expecting to greet the glazier or the locksmith. But the figure in the shaft of dusty sunlight was small and weary-looking, in tight jeans smeared with grass stains, mascara-rimmed eyes, a torn sweatshirt and tangled hair. Her shoulders were slumped and her shoulder purse dangled limply from her fingers. And she just stood there, saying nothing, looking beaten and helpless and frightened.

"Chelsy!" The word escaped through breathless lips, and with it a wash of relief so great, a surge of gratitude so strong, that it left Faith weak. Quickly, she crossed the barren room and took Chelsy's hands, drawing her inside as though afraid she might escape. She was alive, she was unhurt, and she had come back. Something sang inside Faith as she took the small limp hands in hers, something that felt peculiarly like the awakening of joy, a cautious embrace of hope.

Faith looked her over quickly, carefully, concern growing as she noted the white, strained face and the tired eyes. What had happened to the girl in the three days and nights she had been gone, alone and homeless? What had she done, where had she been? Anxiety tightened within Faith as she pushed Chelsy's tangled hair away from her face and whispered, "Oh, honey, are you all right? Do you need a doctor? Have you been hurt or—"

"No." Chelsy shook her head slowly; she even tried to smile. "I'm okay. Just tired. I haven't had much chance to sleep...." The words trailed off as the smudged and bleary eyes filled slowly with tears. Her small figure seemed to crumple and sag, and Faith caught her, holding her, stroking her hair and murmuring senseless soothing words while Chelsy's tears wet her shoulder. She cried quietly, tiredly, for a long time. It was an expiation, a draining and a strengthening, the release of things past that could not be recalled, but in some way the opening of a door onto the future. And in a strange and subtle way, sharing Chelsy's pain, joining in the return of one who was still young enough to have a second chance stirred something deep within Faith. It felt like the flowering of hope.

Chelsy was sitting on the low wooden table that once had held a magnificent spring centerpiece. Faith found her a box of tissues and a cup of water, and every once in a while another sluggish tear would spill down Chelsy's cheek and be absently wiped away with the back of her hand while she shredded the tissues to fine pieces with her fingers.

"I don't know why I came back here," she said thickly, her eyes downcast. "I know I'm in a lot of trouble. What I did..." She gulped. "I guess it was the rottenest thing I've ever done to anybody. We planned it all week, you know, Tony and me...." She tore another corner off the tissue. "We were going to run away together, and the money was so easy to get to...." She looked around the shop in bleak despair. "I didn't know he was going to wreck your place, Miss Hilliard. I really didn't. But he was all bummed out and..." She took a shaky breath. "I guess I should have known."

Chelsy dropped her eyes again. "I felt real bad about it," she admitted. "Those last couple of days...after you were so nice to me and you gave me the necklace and everything..." Her hand moved absently to touch the necklace that she still wore. "But a guy's gotta look out for himself, right? Only...then, that night, he was so messed up, and he wanted to pawn the necklace...." Another fat, slow tear rolled down Chelsy's cheek. Her voice was very small. "Nobody's ever given me anything just because they wanted to before." She took a breath. "And it was just wrong. I didn't want to go with him, I didn't want to do this to you...so I called the police and hoped they would stop him...."

Faith sat back on her heels, watching the girl intently. "You called the police?" she repeated softly.

Chelsy nodded, her eyes still lowered. "Then I split. I was too ashamed, and...scared, I guess...but running away didn't make anything any better because...

well, it just didn't. But anyway." She lifted her face bravely. She took a thick breath. "I had to come back and tell you I was sorry and..." She reached slowly behind her and unfastened the necklace. "I guess you want this back." She placed the piece of jewelry in Faith's hand. "I guess you'd better call the cops now," she said weakly.

Faith looked at it for a long, long time. "You're right, Chelsy," she said at last, quietly. "Running away never makes anything any better."

And then she looked up and smiled, reaching around to refasten the necklace on the girl's neck. "This," she said, "is yours. And I don't know about calling the police...seems to me you're not guilty of anything except phoning in a tip that resulted in the apprehension of a criminal. What I think I should do, though," Faith said, standing up decisively, "is call Mrs. Allen and tell her you're ready to come home. And after you get cleaned up and have a good meal, I expect you back here to help me start putting this place back together. We've got a business to run!"

Chelsy stared at her disbelievingly, her tears drying in her eyes as she stammered, "Y-you mean—you'd take me back—you'd let me work here...?"

The mute wonder that Faith saw in the girl's eyes was like the dawn of a new morning, and Faith disguised her own rush of slow pleasure with a severe tightening of her brows and a brisk, "Do I look like the kind of fool who would let my most valuable employee go two weeks before Mother's Day? We've got work to do here, girl—we're reopening tomorrow!"

And beneath the quick breathless delight that surged into Chelsy's face there was still confusion, reluctance to accept a gift so freely offered. "Do you mean," she ventured hesitantly, "that after what I did—you'd forgive me? You'd take me back? Why?" she insisted. "Why would you do that?"

"She would do that," said a calm male voice behind them, "because she cares about you, and she knows that what you've done in the past doesn't matter. It's what you do in the present that counts."

Though he spoke to Chelsy, Ken looked only at Faith as he came slowly into the room. Faith felt her heart stop, felt the world stop, then leap into abrupt and painfully clear motion and color again as her eyes met his, and held. He was here. He had come. His eyes were filling her, encompassing her, and the sound of his voice was the filling of her lungs with air again, the pulsing of life into her veins again, the opening of her eyes after a long sleep.

The moment was too brief, too filled with other things, to be captured or analyzed. Ken moved to Chelsy, and he smiled. "Welcome home, Chelsy," he said gently, and opened his arms to her.

The embrace was quick and intense, and it brought tears to Faith's eyes. This man, with an endless capacity for love and understanding, this beautiful, tender man, who was all that life was meant to be—how could she ever stop loving him? How could she even try?

Ken held Chelsy by the shoulders, looking down at her for a quiet affectionate moment, then he brought his hand up and ruffled her hair playfully. "You had us worried, you renegade," he said huskily. "You okay?"

Chelsy nodded mutely.

"Good." Ken released her with a grin and a quick light shove on the arm that pointed her in the direction of the back room. "Because when you get home, you're in for a sermon the likes of which you've never heard. Right now, go wash your face and comb your hair, then call Mrs. Allen and tell her where you are." And already his eyes were straying toward Faith. "I want to talk to Miss Hilliard for a minute."

Weakness engulfed Faith when they were alone, and she had to reach behind her, hoping for a chair, finding only the wall for support. She could hear her heart rushing and waning in her ears, and everything within her was honed and pinpointed on this moment—alert, waiting, concentrating on his next words, trying very hard not to hope.

But for a moment Ken said nothing. His eyes roamed around the room, noticing, as she had, the bleakness and the emptiness of it. Soon his feet followed and he moved to pick up the wicker basket she had dropped, sweeping up a scattering of straw flowers on the floor, circling to drop them in the trash can at her feet. And then he looked at her.

There was a quick flash of uncertainty far back in his eyes, a gentle hesitancy, but overriding it a deep searching, a quiet desperation, and the effort it took for him to form a brief smile seemed enormous. "Well," he said softly, "looks like we won one this time, doesn't it?"

But had they? What had they won? Faith could not keep the fear out of her eyes.

Faith saw the tightening of his jaw muscle, the quick flash of something that looked like anger in his eyes, and the faint flutterings of life that had begun in the pit of her stomach abruptly stilled. It felt like an incision directly to the core of her heart.

"All right," he said shortly, eyes narrowing. "I was upset." The words were clipped, his lips tight. "I was shocked. I had a right to be. What did you expect from me?"

Faith closed her eyes slowly in acquiescence. It was the only answer she could give him. She felt a thin stream of breath flutter through her lips, but nothing else. All right. She could accept this. She could accept it and go on, because she had no choice....

And when next he spoke his voice had gentled somewhat, and when she made herself look at him the only anger she saw was directed at himself. "But not," he said, "because of what you told me. Because of the way you said it."

And slowly his face softened, his eyes deepened with tenderness and regret; his hand came up slowly as though to touch her. "Because I could see the pain, because I could imagine what you had been through—both before the DeFrancis scandal and afterward—and because there was nothing, nothing I could do to erase those scars, or ease the pain. Faith—" his hands reached her face, touching it lightly, first with just the back of his knuckles, then turning it into the lightest of cupping caresses "—I love you," he said softly, "for everything you are and everything you have been, past and present, all of you. If you could accept me the way I am—for myself alone and nothing else—whatever made you think I couldn't love you for the same reason?''

The slow and subtle movement Faith heard in her ears was the sound of her heart, beating again. The cool slow dizziness was breath expanding her lungs again, and the sweet wonder that filled her was love, only love. Her lips parted helplessly, she turned them to meet his palm, and the sound that caught in her throat was a sob. Then she was in his arms, muscles straining, hands groping, bodies pressing; breaths suspended and rushing, tears dampening his neck and his collar, hearts thudding and bursting to beat as one.

His hands stroked her hair unsteadily, his lips brushed across her wet lashes, at last his fingers tightened around her skull and he tilted her head back a little, looking at her intently. ''Faith,'' he said softly, unevenly, ''don't you think I know what kind of courage it took for you to survive that kind of life—the strength it took to walk away and build a new life for yourself? Darling…'' His eyes moved over her face, drinking of her, drawing of her, touching every feature as though to imprint it on his memory. He pushed her hair away from her forehead, wanting to see all of her, wanting to know all of her. ''I know there's more you have to tell me, more I want to understand, about what went on in that period of your life. But don't you know that it's that strength, that courage, that I need from you … that I can't live without—''

But she had to say it. She could not let him go into this blindly, to give his life away for her. "What about your congregation?" she insisted in a whisper, searching his eyes painfully. "What about the scandal?"

He smiled gently. "I've survived scandal before," he assured her. "And my congregation, if they've learned anything at all from me these past three years, will understand." His hand came up, lightly stroking her face; his eyes sobered. "It won't be easy," he said. "But then, nothing worth having ever is."

And then his mouth was on hers and she was rising to meet him, accepting and giving to him greedily, thirstily, time without end. Faith knew and recognized at last the power of that Unseen Hand that had from the beginning been leading them to this moment, and she welcomed its presence with all her heart and all her soul. Neither had ever had a choice in the matter. None at all.

"An answer," he demanded at last, huskily, his eyes bright and glowing and deep with an inner conviction she could not resist, had never been able to resist.

"Yes," she whispered, and the radiance in her own eyes matched his. Just as it was always meant to be. "Yes..."

His lashes dropped slowly on the depth of utter contentment; a wondering smile curved his lips. But when he looked at her he knew that it was true; when Faith looked at him she saw right into his soul.

They held each other for a long time, breaths mingling, hearts opening, eyes giving and receiving promises and assurances that no amount of time could threaten. And then Ken smiled and reached around her to open the cooler door. From the bottom shelf he drew a single white rose.

"For eternity," he said softly, and placed it in her hand.

Epilogue

It was a June wedding. The church was filled with wild-flowers gathered by the children from the Crossroads and arranged by Chelsy's expert hand to outshine anything Faith could have designed with the most elaborate budget. Every pew was filled, and mingling with the well-dressed members of Ken's congregation in their chiffons, flowered hats and three-piece suits was a lively collection of teenagers in jeans and polo shirts, every one of whom needed a haircut. It was the most wonderful, welcoming crowd Faith had ever seen, and Ken stood at the head of it all. Only this time he did not hold a prayer book in his hands. He simply waited for Faith.

Faith's gown was a natural muslin with a princess waistline and leg-of-mutton sleeves; her hair was loose, the way Ken liked it, and adorned with streamers of baby's breath and cherry blossoms. She carried a bouquet of pink, red and white roses. There was nothing traditional about the ceremony, but neither was there anything traditional about the two people whose lives it would join.

Chelsy, in a lavender print gown and a wide-brimmed straw hat, proceeded down the aisle before her, looking as mature and in control as if this were her own wedding day. And Faith, taking the arm of her proud and approving father, felt not a single quaver of nervousness as she began her own procession. All she saw was Ken.

Before the altar, Faith's father placed her hand in Ken's. The guest minister stood patiently by, and Ken looked at her for a long, long time. In his eyes, Faith saw strength and security, and more love than she ever thought possible... more than she surely deserved. She would spend the rest of her life returning that love to him.

Ken touched her cheek lightly and slowly he smiled. "Do you remember?" he said softly. "I told you I would marry you. Maybe from now on you'll believe what I say."

Faith returned his smile. She couldn't help it—more happiness than she had ever imagined was bubbling through from every part of her soul, and she had to smile. She released his hand briefly, and she glanced down to gently extract a white rose from her bouquet.

She looked at the rose for a moment, then at Ken. Her eyes were glowing from deep within, her smile a promise for all the future. "I believe," she said softly, and she placed the rose in his hand.

Harlequin

INDULGE IN THE PLEASURE OF SUPERB ROMANCE READING BY CHOOSING THE MOST POPULAR LOVE STORIES IN THE WORLD

Longer, more absorbing love stories for the connoisseur of romantic fiction.

Contemporary romances— uniquely North American in flavor and appeal.

An innovative series blending contemporary romance with fast-paced adventure.

and you can never have too much romance.

Share the joys and sorrows
of real-life love with
Harlequin American Romance!™

GET THIS BOOK
FREE as your introduction to
Harlequin American Romance — an exciting series of romance novels written especially for the American woman of today.

Mail to:
Harlequin Reader Service

In the U.S.
2504 West Southern Ave.
Tempe, AZ 85282

In Canada
P.O. Box 2800, Postal Station A
5170 Yonge St., Willowdale, Ont. M2N 6J3

YES! I want to be one of the first to discover
Harlequin American Romance. Send me FREE and without obligation *Twice in a Lifetime*. If you do not hear from me after I have examined my FREE book, please send me the 4 new **Harlequin American Romances** each month as soon as they come off the presses. I understand that I will be billed only $2.25 for each book (total $9.00). There are no shipping or handling charges. There is no minimum number of books that I have to purchase. In fact, I may cancel this arrangement at any time. *Twice in a Lifetime* is mine to keep as a FREE gift, even if I do not buy any additional books.   154-BPA-NAZJ

Name _____ (please print)

Address _____ Apt. no. _____

City _____ State/Prov. _____ Zip/Postal Code _____

Signature (If under 18, parent or guardian must sign.)

This offer is limited to one order per household and not valid to current Harlequin American Romance subscribers. We reserve the right to exercise discretion in granting membership. If price changes are necessary, you will be notified.

AMR-SUB-1R

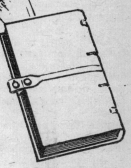